T
UNSCHEDULED MURDER TRIP
ELAINE L. ORR

Copyright © 2021 Elaine L. Orr

Lifelong Dreams Publishing

All rights reserved.

No part of this publication may be reproduced, distributed, or transmitted in any form or by any means, including photocopying, recording, or other electronic or mechanical methods except as permitted by U.S. copyright law.

ISBN-13: 978-1-948070-72-0

Library of Congress Preassigned Control Number: 2021901734

THE UNSCHEDULED MURDER TRIP
ELAINE L. ORR

Book 2 of the

Family History Mystery Series

The Unscheduled Murder Trip is a work of fiction.

All characters and story lines are products of the author's imagination.

elaineorr.com

elaineorr.blogspot.com

DEDICATION

*To my family and the friends
who are as close as family.*

ACKNOWLEDGMENTS

The fictional settings of my books are based on places I know fairly well, though the towns are always my own creation. I'll mention real towns to give readers a frame of reference.

For the Family History Mystery Series, I chose the Western Maryland Mountains of Garrett County, because I love to drive through there as I travel from my current home in the Midwest to visit family in Maryland. I especially love taking the train through the region. Maple Grove is my creation, though characters spend time in the real county seat (Oakland) and visit a couple of other small towns. However, my April 2020 research trip went the way of all discretionary travel in the year of COVID. Because I could not visit, I especially appreciated books I bought from the Garrett County Historical Society. They include "Ghost Towns of the Upper Potomac" (compiled by the Society) and "Garrett County: A History of Maryland's Tableland" by Stephen Schlosnagle and the Garrett County Bicentennial Committee. I also used "The Western Maryland Railway" by Anthony Puzzilla, and a number of articles found on the Internet. I look forward to a visit to the region in 2021. As always, I appreciate the members of the Decatur critique group – Angela, Dave, and both Sues

BOOKS IN THE FAMILY HISTORY MYSTERY SERIES

Least Trodden Ground
Unscheduled Murder Trip
Mountain Rails of Old
Gilded Path to Nowhere

Jolie Gentil Mystery Series
Appraisal for Murder
Rekindling Motives
When the Carny Comes to Town
Any Port in a Storm
Trouble on the Doorstep
Behind the Walls
Vague Images
Ground to a Halt
Holidays in Ocean Alley
The Unexpected Resolution
The Twain Does Meet (novella)
Underground in Ocean Alley
Aunt Madge in the Civil Election (an Aunt Madge story)
Sticky Fingered Books
New Lease on Death
Jolie and Scoobie High School Misadventures (prequel)

River's Edge Series — *set in rural Iowa*
Logland Series — *set in small-town Illinois*

Books are at online retailers, or ask your library or bookstore to order them — in print, large print, ebook and audio. All books have Barnes and Noble editions, which makes them easy to order from those stores.

CHAPTER ONE

November 23, 1963

DANIEL STEVENS LOVED THE mountains of Western Maryland. His family had lived in Garrett County since the first land grants after the Revolutionary War. The only time he'd left for anything other than short vacations was to serve in World War II.

He fought hard to protect his country then. His wife said, in her gentle way, that he left his better nature on the shores of Omaha Beach. But it wasn't enough. Yesterday, someone had killed his president in Dallas.

He stared into his beer and muttered, "Everything we fought for, and they kill the president in our own country."

The bartender walked toward him. "Need something, Daniel?"

"No thanks, Harrison." He nodded toward the black-and-white television that sat on a platform above the line of multi-colored bottles of liquor. "Just wishing that never happened."

"Me, too. I didn't vote for the guy, but I sure didn't wish him dead." Harrison returned to his spot at the corner of the bar, where he often stood to greet arriving customers. Fewer tonight because of the crummy weather.

When he was sure the bartender was too far away to read the piece of paper Daniel pulled from his pocket, he studied the handwritten figures he'd been puzzling over. He couldn't make heads or tails of them.

Daniel and his business partner operated Mountain Granite Quarry, and Daniel was the face to the customers. Given their location at the nexus of three states, some days Daniel had meetings in Maryland, West Virginia, and Pennsylvania. He never minded driving through the mountains. Unless the roads were slick. Like tonight.

THE UNSCHEDULED MURDER TRIP

He made a decent living. Isabella ran the dairy farm Daniel had inherited from his parents. He had no interest in farming, whether cows or corn.

That's why he jumped at the chance to partner with Harlan Jones. They were like half the vets Daniel knew – heck, almost all of them in Garret County. They'd been part of something important and returned to small towns to resume their lives. Resume, but with a lot of memories he'd rather not have.

In the feed store where Harlan worked, one day they had commiserated about how hard it was to keep gravel on the mountain roads. Every spring, rural roads would be mud and the county had to spread more gravel. The two men never debated whose idea it was to make an offer for the floundering Mountain Granite Quarry. It was as if they both saw opportunity in a business that supplied a basic need.

Building the quarry into a flourishing business had given them purpose. Eisenhower's National Defense Highway Act brought them a lot of customers. Most of the interstate highway system in the area had gravel shoulders. Daniel and Harlan had the stone to sell to Uncle Sam and his contractors.

When Harlan and his wife, Felicia, built their six-bedroom home in the hamlet of Bloomington, Maryland, Daniel couldn't imagine why they wanted to live in such a small town, but he had been happy for them. Sure, the death of Harlan's Uncle Charles was sad, but the old guy would have been pleased that the money he left for his nephew and family was put to good use.

Except Daniel had just learned, by chance, really, that there'd been no inheritance. He'd run into Charles' widow over in Martinsburg. Daniel had been in West Virginia to talk to a medical practice about stone for the grounds at a new building, and she'd been in the waiting room.

Because she and Charles had left Maple Grove years ago, he hadn't seen her since her husband died. When he'd commented that he expected she missed him, she'd said yes, but joked that what she really missed was living in a household with two Social Security checks. One was hard to stretch.

Daniel held back any surprise. Surely if Harlan's uncle had left him a 'tidy sum' he would have provided for his wife as well.

His and Harlan's families had very different lifestyles. The Jones always had new cars and made a point of donating enough to the United Way to be mentioned in the annual fundraising brochure.

Daniel and Isabella got by fine, but regular new car purchases were out of the question, to say nothing of a huge home. Daniel had always assumed that a lot of the money he earned went to operate the dairy farm. Isabella managed their finances, and that was fine with him.

He didn't want to appear to question financial decisions Isabella made, so he suggested to her that they make sure their small retirement funds were invested well. She pulled out the farm and family books and Daniel learned his income didn't subsidize the farm. It more or less paid for itself and his quarry income supported their family. No complaints.

But if Harlan and he paid themselves the same salaries, why did Harlan have so much more to spend? Or so it seemed.

Daniel was no accountant, but his favorite subject in school was math. He had helped Isabella so she didn't flunk geometry.

Yesterday he had gone to the Garrett County courthouse and looked up the real estate records for the house Harlan and Felicia sold and the value of the one they built. They'd barely made a profit on the two-story home they sold in Maple Grove.

The Bloomington house was valued at more than $100,000, and had to have a mortgage. Harlan had quietly confided that his uncle's bequest let them pay cash for some of the construction costs. But that seemed to be a lie.

Daniel took a swig of his beer, an ingestion of confidence. Harlan and Felicia had gone to Pittsburgh to do some Christmas shopping this weekend. They'd be home tomorrow, Sunday, so there was no chance Harlan would drive to Maple Grove this evening. Even if he were home, slick roads would keep him in Bloomington.

Daniel would drive to the quarry office and have a more detailed look at financial records. He reviewed the annual reports every year and could recite any information about the company's

THE UNSCHEDULED MURDER TRIP

worth and cash flow. But Harlan was the inside man while Daniel handled new business and customer service. He'd never freely roamed through the files. He would tonight.

With a nod to Harrison, Daniel put three dollars on the bar and headed for his car. When he saw the fresh, thin layer of ice on his windshield he almost changed his mind. But he couldn't. This was his chance to spend time going over records without anyone asking why he was more interested than usual.

He warmed up the car while he used an ice scraper on the windshield. He really should go home. But he couldn't.

Daniel drove slowly out of the parking lot and his car slid as he crossed in front of the old train depot. Back in the day, a spur ran from Maple Grove to Cumberland, Maryland. He'd boarded a train there to leave for the war.

The quarry was higher up Meadow Mountain than the bar, and Daniel drove at a steady pace. Not too fast and not too slow, so his car wouldn't spin out. If the ice wasn't such a pain, he'd enjoy looking at the icicles it created on the evergreen trees.

Not a single car came toward him or drove behind him. Anyone with any sense was indoors with hot tea or a stiff drink.

He planned to spend about an hour at the firm. Isabella thought he had gone to a Knights of Columbus meeting at the church social hall. It ended roughly at nine o'clock. He needed to be home by nine-thirty or shortly after.

Daniel didn't usually fib to his wife, but he didn't want to bother her with his suspicions unless they became reality. She worried about the farm, cows about to calf, and their kids. He chuckled. Almost in that order.

He parked in the visitor spot by Mountain Granite Quarry's admin building. Snow had gotten heavy enough that he could barely see to the first quarry pit a few hundred yards away. He fumbled with his keys. It was supposed to snow in earnest by midnight. He probably shouldn't have come.

When he got inside, Daniel turned the thermostat up two degrees to take the chill out of the air. He'd have to remember to turn it down when he left. He considered not turning lights on in the reception area, but he wasn't hiding what he was doing. Except maybe from Harlan.

Six file cabinets sat along the wall of the room used for making mimeographs and designing sales copy. He didn't want to sit in the enclosed room, so he carried the files to the maple table in the corner of the reception area.

Daniel wanted to compare receipts for purchases and income from their larger clients. He didn't expect to find obvious evidence of embezzlement – there, he'd put the word formally in his brain – but that had to be a place to start.

Except obvious was the operative word. Harlan regularly paid Handy Equipment Company for upgrades to their small fleet of dump trucks, backhoes, front-end loaders, dozers, and company cars. He also paid a pretty penny for vehicle maintenance. But the quarry did not have that many vehicles, and most were several years old. While well maintained, they didn't get monthly tune-ups or alignments, which is what some invoices indicated.

Daniel realized that Harlan set up Handy Equipment Company so he could expense some of the quarry's income. The post office box for Handy Equipment was likely one Harlan maintained. No one would question a firm's use of a postal box.

As a private company, no board of directors paid attention to finances. The Internal Revenue Service would never know enough to question Harlan's scheme, and the financial reports Daniel saw didn't reflect the payments to Handy Equipment. Harlan had an extra thousand dollars per month, a sum that could easily cover a large mortgage.

Aloud he said, "That scheming SOB."

He leaned forward so his nose almost touched the statement of net worth. His head didn't have far to travel when the excruciating pain behind his neck propelled him forward.

CHAPTER TWO

Present day

DIGGER BROWNING CLOSED the door of the Ancestral Sanctuary as quietly as she could. She'd oiled the hinges herself last week, so her exits would be quieter. To anyone who believed she and her two pets lived alone, tiptoeing out of her house might seem odd. To anyone who wondered why she had taken to muttering to herself, it could seem like just another quirky habit.

She eased herself into the Jeep's driver's seat, fastened her seatbelt, and started the car. Sneaking out had gotten easier with practice, but it would be tough when she had to scrape the car's windows.

At the end of the long driveway she turned left, heading down to Maple Grove and the business – You Think, We Design – which she and her friend Holly had started three months ago.

The man's voice from the back seat caused Digger to jerk the steering wheel to the left, narrowly missing her neighbors' mail stand.

"If you really want to avoid me you should walk out in your stocking feet."

"Uncle Benjamin! I told you not to scare me when I'm driving."

"If you'd tell me when you were leaving, I wouldn't have to."

Digger backed the car away from the mailbox and continued driving. "I told you last night, I have a lot to do. I don't have time for editorial comments all day."

The apparition in the back seat huffed. *"A consultant usually makes good money. You don't have to pay me a dime."*

She kept herself from smiling. When her late, great uncle appeared in the kitchen the day of his funeral, she had been shocked, but not unhappy. It felt like getting a second chance with the octogenarian. Digger loved him and had lots of family history questions she hadn't asked.

Now, however, the fact that he appeared at any time and rattled around the large house had grown old. So could his ability to follow her anywhere. So old that she tried to lose him some mornings, since he could only go to town if he left with her.

The crafty son-of-a-gun had developed a sixth sense about her whereabouts. Or maybe apparitions had ten senses. She didn't plan to find out.

"Can I pay you not to talk?"

"Maybe if I find a ghost bank somewhere. What are we doing today?"

"Holly and I are going to discuss plans for the brochure for the Visitor's Center, and I'm going over to the old train depot to take some pictures of it before the renovations start. Did you notice the pronouns?"

"Exclusionary. Very rude."

Digger turned onto Crooked Leg Road, toward town. "I really need you not to yammer in my ear all the time. Holly's starting to think I'm losing my mind."

"Then tell her you've gained a second perspective."

Digger didn't respond. Late fall in the Western Maryland mountains was her favorite season. But when frost came overnight, the narrow road had deceptive surprises. With snow, or even ice, you could see the road was slick. With early-morning frost, there was an almost invisible sheen.

"What about...?" Uncle Benjamin began.

"I need to concentrate."

As she grew closer to the hardware store at the base of the long hill, the road offered better traction. Even a small town's activities could add enough warmth to dissipate the frost on the road.

Her thoughts turned to design work for You Think, We Design's best customer. Mountain Granite Quarry had been her client when she worked for her former employer, but her boss hadn't thought to develop contracts that required graphic artists to stay away from their former clients if they left the firm.

In fact, when Western Maryland Ad Agency laid off Digger and Holly, the quarry had sought them out. Stufflebeam, her old boss, had tried to woo back one of his firm's larger clients, but the quarry rebuffed him. Digger had to endure Stufflebeam's snide comments if she passed him in the grocery store, but she could do that for their bread-and-butter client.

Lights came on in their second-story office as Digger pulled into a parking space. Holly passed in front of the window. She grabbed her backpack and shut the car door firmly.

"You can't lock me in, you know."

"A woman can try," she said.

Digger jogged up the stairs to the landing and then to the second-floor hallway. At some point, an earlier tenant had refinished the hardwood stairs and hallway, which were more than one hundred years old. When she and Holly rented the space, they had gotten permission to repaint the short hallway beige, as well as the interior of their office. The result was a pleasing combination of old and new.

Downtown Maple Grove had a colorful mix of two-and-three story brick and frame buildings, many of them visible from their office windows. Much of the town lay below them, and the mountain rose again from this small valley. The blended shades of orange and yellow had been spectacular this year, but now largely bare trees dotted the landscape.

Stuck to the glass portion of the office door, just under the firm's name, was a 5x7 brown envelope with her name on it. Digger grabbed it and walked in. "Good morning."

Holly's voice came from the corner of the office that they referred to as the kitchen. "I'm making coffee. Do you have a secret admirer?"

"That'll be the day."

"If there's a check in here I'll let everyone know." She placed the envelope on the corner of her desk and turned to join Holly. "Oh, my God! What happened to your cornrows?"

Her partner made a graceful half-bow. "What do you think?" When Digger said nothing, she frowned. "You don't like it?"

"It looks terrific. Really frames your face."

"Too round. Makes her face look fat."

Holly touched her short Afro lightly. "I decided to go au naturel. Cornrows sort of were, but nothing says proud Black woman like a natural hairstyle."

"True." Digger smiled. "And you did it just before we had our promo pictures taken."

Holly took a sip of her coffee. "Grandma Audrey gets the credit. I'd been trying to get up the nerve, and when I mentioned we had the photo shoot appointment, she said if I didn't do it before that I'd have to wait a good while."

"Smart woman. Trade places." Holly's new cut reminded her she should probably get her long hair either styled for the promo photos, or have someone else do her French braid that day.

Holly moved away from the coffee machine and Digger grabbed her mug and put a hazelnut pod in the basket. "I'm going to take some pictures at the depot before they start any work. Want to come?"

"No. I'm going over to the alterations place on Allegheny Street."

"Buy something new?"

"No. I think their signage is terrible. I'm going to see if Jack and Alice will let me design something better."

Digger nodded. "That's great. A lot of people go in there. Maybe they'll ask who did the work."

"I'm counting on it." Holly picked up a sketch pad and charcoal pencil from her desk and began drawing.

"Still looks like doodling to me."

For the umpteenth time, Digger wished she had a telepathic link with Uncle Benjamin. Then she could tell him to put a cork in his mouth without anyone else hearing her. She finished pouring coffee into her new mug, a gift from her friend Marty Hofstedder. It had a single tombstone and the words 'Genealogists love their rounds.'

Digger gravitated to her L-shaped desk and raised the shade so she could see the fall panorama in the distance. Steeples of the Methodist and Catholic churches, the tallest landmarks, stood sentry over the town of 3,000.

THE UNSCHEDULED MURDER TRIP

Part of the renovation project that would turn the vacant train depot into a visitors' center involved writing town history in varied lengths – short for a tourist brochure, longer for a booklet to sell at various merchants, and in-depth for a pictorial history. Uncle Benjamin and his friends at the historical society had collected hundreds of old photos, and Digger's job was to capture current conditions.

After a second swig of coffee, she opened the brown envelope and unfolded the piece of yellow legal paper.

Dear Ms. Browning,

We haven't met. I'm Brian Stevens, and my parents are Matthew and Sylvia. You may have heard my dad has cancer. He'll be around for a year or two (I hope), and I'd like to find out what happened to his father, Daniel Stevens.

My grandmother, Isabella, came to believe he deserted her and my dad. The more I learn about him, the less I think that. Obviously, neither you or I can prove what happened in 1963. But you know how to trace people. I don't really want to learn that he left here and started a second family out west or something, but if that's what he did, I'd rather my father have the peace of knowing what happened.

Can we meet at the historical society, or could I buy you a cup of coffee at The Coffee Engine?
Sincerely,
Brian Stevens

He'd included his phone number and email, and Digger studied them for several seconds before facing Holly, who wore an expectant expression.

"Not a secret admirer. But there is a connection to Mountain Granite Quarry. Have you heard about Daniel Stevens, the man who vanished in the early 1960s?"

"Vaguely familiar. Drove out for a beer or something and never got home?"

"I sure as hell remember him."

Digger scratched her cheek with her middle finger, hoping it was within Uncle Benjamin's line of sight. "My uncle knew him from the VFW. He thought Daniel Stevens had what we now call PTSD, but said he really loved his wife and two kids. He was in World War II, so he was maybe ten or more years older than Uncle Benjamin."

Holly nodded toward Digger's hand, which held the notebook sheet. "So, this letter is about him?"

"From his grandson. He wants me to help him find out if his grandfather had a second life somewhere. It would give his dad, Matthew, some resolution."

"Ask him if he's sure he wants to open that can of worms."

"Like hire you?"

"Hardly. He did say he'd buy me a cup of coffee. I can show him what kinds of records to search, but I'm not holding his hand." She turned back to her desk. "I'm going to do some design work for Mountain Granite's sales brochure before I go to the depot."

"Wait, what about Stevens and the quarry?" Holly asked.

"He owned it with the Jones family, or something like that. There's a picture of him on the wall in the reception area."

CHAPTER THREE

DIGGER PULLED INTO THE RUTTED parking area next to the two-story, brick train depot. She wanted to get some exterior photos before noon. Then she'd head inside to capture the distinctive mullioned windows and remaining old benches while there was good light. She'd brought some battery-operated lighting, but the more natural light the better.

Before she got out of the car, she changed to the work boots she used when doing yard work or cleaning the small cemetery plot at the Ancestral Sanctuary. The ground wasn't too soggy, but beer bottles sometimes littered the area closest to the depot.

A visual survey revealed that volunteers had cleared away a lot of brush. Several stacks of shingles, cleverly concealed under a bright blue tarp, reminded Digger that work to repair the roof was to begin in the next day or two.

"What are you waiting for?"

Digger opened her car door. "Train to Martinsburg."

"Hasn't run for more than forty years."

"I have to concentrate. Please don't tell history tidbits the entire time I'm shooting."

"My extensive historical knowledge does not present itself in tidbits."

She ignored him and unloaded the lighting equipment and slung the camera strap over her shoulder. She walked past the resilient board that had displayed the timetables, a sundial that had been vandalized years ago, and the remaining portions of the sign that had once said Maple Grove and now said Mo Gr, the middle portion having collapsed just a short time ago.

She took the key for the padlock out of the pocket of her slacks, and set her two battery-operated lanterns on the ground while she unlocked the building. The door creaked open, revealing an interior that was cleaner than when she'd been in more than a year ago. The historical society hadn't left it deliberately dirty, but the packing process had been hectic.

Today, two long brooms stood in a corner next to a trash can and large dustpan. Some of the lower windowpanes had been cleaned so sun came in from several directions. Good for lighting when sweeping, but the unevenness of sunlight might not be good for the pictures she would take.

From the other side of the depot, Uncle Benjamin called, *"They'll have to pull up all the floor on the second story. Those water leaks right after the historical society moved out did a lot of damage."*

Digger studied the rickety stairs to the locked second floor. They didn't look as if they would bear even her 110 pounds. She placed her canvas bag on a bench and removed the camera and its versatile lens.

Sunlight played on the corner of the bench farthest from her, which she liked. The glare on the windows wasn't helpful, so she took shots from different parts of the room.

Finally, she was ready for exterior photos.

"Took you long enough."

Maybe positive reinforcement would work. "Thank you for not interrupting me."

The temperature had dropped a couple of degrees and the wind had come up. Digger sniffed. The air definitely smelled as if winter lurked nearby.

She almost stumbled in a rut because she had looked through the lens instead of where she walked. If she hadn't had on the work boots, she'd have sprained her ankle.

Irritated, she glanced down and saw a couple of pieces of colorful fabric on the ground. She picked up the red and gold fabric and decided the scraps had been part of an old carpet. None of the depot photos showed any carpeting, but maybe there had been some behind the ticket counter.

She pocketed them. If she found pictures with this color carpet, she could put these in the display case that was going to depict the renovations.

"I don't remember any carpet."

Digger started. "Jeez, Uncle Benjamin, I've asked you not to sneak up on me."

"Sorry. You want me to give you a guided tour now that you're done with your picture-taking?"

"I'll be done in a minute, but no thanks. I have to get back to the office."

As she pulled out her keys, an almost elegant-looking, white SUV pulled into the lot and parked at the far side. She didn't know the car, but recognized its occupant, Leon Jones. She was surprised to see one of the owners of Mountain Granite Quarry at the deserted depot.

He raised a hand in greeting. "Didn't expect to see you Digger. What are you up to?"

"Taking pictures for the Chamber, and me, to use when the visitors' center opens."

Jones walked toward her. "Similar timeframe. Did you know we provided gravel for this parking lot forty or so years ago, and will again?"

"Who cares?"

"Gosh no. You bringing more in soon?"

Jones stopped a few feet from her. "No, just sort of eyeballing the area to get a sense of what we'll need. My folks will measure later."

"Do you have any photos of you guys spreading the gravel back then?"

"Don't think so, but there was a newspaper article about some of our equipment getting stuck in the mud. Funny shot of my dad raising his hands in exasperation. Want me to try to find it?"

Digger shook her head. "If I can't come up with it at the historical society, I'll let you know. Maybe you can use a couple of this year's pictures in your annual report or something?"

His eyebrows went up. "Good idea. Send your rates for something like that."

She smiled. "No charge for our best client. I'd appreciate a photo credit if you use any."

"Done." Jones turned toward the depot itself. "My parents, mostly my mom, talked about how great it was to take the train from here. I have some memory of us taking it down to Cumberland and transferring to go to Washington, DC to look at the cherry blossoms one year."

"Clara and I did that, too. Train got stopped by rocks on the tracks and we had to wait two hours to move again."

"I think Uncle Benjamin and Aunt Clara did that, too."

"Copycat."

Jones shook his head. "Shame he had to die like that. How are you getting on now that you own his old place?"

"Mostly I miss him, but I love being out there. It's a beautiful old house."

"Mostly?"

Jones surveyed the area again. "We'll probably have to move that old sundial. It's made of limestone, and cracked. Not sure it'll survive being uprooted."

"Do you know who stole the dial years ago?"

He shook his head. "Don't think anyone does. Lots of folks upset. It was kind of a tourist attraction."

"I always wondered why it sat almost in the parking lot."

Jones shook his head. "Originally that spot was a small garden. When they wanted to expand the lot, the railroad hired us to put in more gravel."

"I'm surprised it never got run over."

"Used to be a short metal fence separating that spot from the parking spaces. Put up after someone almost hit the sundial."

"The old mayor's wife backed into it. She thought her car was in forward and it was in reverse. Lucky she was such a slowpoke."

Digger took in Leon's black, wool topcoat and erect posture as he surveyed the area. He had to be at least seventy-five. "Are you enjoying having your daughter join the business?"

"Very much. Marilyn didn't plan to be so involved in the quarry, but the recession changed life for a lot of people. Her husband isn't from here, of course, but now that they've moved here, he appreciates the town."

THE UNSCHEDULED MURDER TRIP

Digger had heard that Marilyn's husband, Tony Davis, had fallen in love with Maple Grove. She tilted her head toward the car. "I need to get back to our office so Holly can head out for some other work."

"You two like being downtown?"

"We love it. We can walk to the Coffee Engine."

He laughed. "Better fuel than coal for the old steam engines."

"Agreed. Talk to you later." Digger moved to her car and put the equipment in the trunk. When she slid behind the engine and started the car, Uncle Benjamin made his presence known."

"You know, if you left me someplace, I think I could walk back to the Ancestral Sanctuary. Not like I'd get blisters."

"You can walk or float. Couldn't you fly back?"

"I'm not a fruit bat. Or maybe I could jump off the roof of the depot and see if I can force myself to fly."

"I'm going back to the office. Don't you want to take a nap in the car or something?"

"I'm the first person who took you to Gettysburg, you know."

She smiled. "And you told dad me getting a history degree wasn't such a bad thing."

"So mind your manners."

Digger pulled in front of their building. "I really need to concentrate on work for a couple of hours. Please don't jibber jabber."

As she closed the car door, she made eye contact with a man in his early twenties, who wore a puzzled expression.

"Are you Digger Browning?" He glanced into the back seat of her Jeep.

She studied his compact frame and sandy blonde hair, and smiled. "I am. Who might you be?"

"I'm Brian Stevens. I left you a note this morning."

"I got it, and planned to call you this afternoon."

"Thanks." He walked behind her as she moved up the stairs. "I don't mean to rush you, but I want to help my dad know what happened to his father. The more I look into it, the more I think he may have been killed."

CHAPTER FOUR

DIGGER STOPPED ON THE LANDING and stared at Brian Stevens on the step below. "That's a strong thing to say."

He flushed. "I know. I've been interviewing people who knew him. I mean, my grandmother's dead, but other people aren't."

"Who have you talked to?"

Brian shuffled through papers. "I have a list. My Aunt Carol in Colorado, of course. She never comes home, so that was on the phone. She barely remembers Daniel, but said if he took her to work, or anywhere, everyone joked with him and told him she was cute."

"Your grandfather's friends would likely be dead, right?"

"A couple old guys at the Knights of Columbus were in their twenties when he...vanished. They said he was quiet, but was the first guy you could ask for a favor." Brian smiled. "One of them had an old car back then, and Daniel jump started it for him like five times, and then gave him twenty-five dollars to get a new battery."

"That does sound like a good guy."

"I liked what I saw of him."

Brian shook his head. "It doesn't make sense. Everyone says the same thing. He never would have left his family."

It sounded more like a hopeful thought than true information, but Digger got where he was coming from. "I see. Well, come on up. We have a coffee pot." She turned and began climbing again.

"You want a cup at the Coffee Engine? My treat."

"I like that place. You should take him up on it."

Digger gestured that Brian should enter the office before she did. "Not sure you'd want everyone hearing our conversation."

Holly looked up from her draft board as they entered. "Now that'd be a good opening line for a play. Or maybe a book."

"Brian Stevens, this is my partner, Holly."

Brian waved from across the room and pulled up his mask. "You don't need to get up." He stood perpendicular to the front window, so he could look sideways to each of them. "I saw that article in the *Maple Grove News* about you two opening this business last month. Hope you don't mind that I just come by."

Digger pointed to a chair next to her desk. "No problem. I'll give you my email in a minute so you can check before you come next time. Save you a trip if I'm out."

That was a good way to tell him not to come by unannounced.

As he sat, Digger met Holly's eyes. She did a half-shoulder-shrug before she went back to her work.

Digger swiveled in her chair to face him. "So, Brian, I'm sorry your dad's sick. What is it you want to do?"

"Okay." He took a breath. "In November 1963, my grandfather left home, supposedly to go to a Knights of Columbus meeting."

"Those guys know how to drink beer."

"But instead, he had a drink at a bar. Later the bartender said he was kind of muttering to himself, but they didn't really talk. And that's the last anyone ever heard of him."

She found his earnest expression under dark black hair almost painful to see. How could he find out something no one had discovered for decades? "That must have been hard on your dad and grandmother."

"My dad, he's Matthew, said my grandmother was frantic for days. People looked everywhere for him."

"No word at all?"

Brian shook his head. "Nothing. The people at the *News* told me I could get the newspaper on microfilm at the historical society, so I read all the articles. They searched everywhere, not just on the mountain. I guess the sheriff, a lot of people, figured he might have gone off the road, and the snow hid his car."

"So, bad weather that night?"

"Yeah. Worse than expected. Almost a foot of snow by morning. Dad said the sheriff kind of thought when the snow melted, they'd find his car in a bunch of pine trees halfway down the mountain, but they didn't."

"So…you want me to do what?"

I read the letter. You get to be his tutor.

"Because he's dying, my dad's talked more about it lately. He always wondered if his father thought everything was just too much and left. They used to go fishing every year on his birthday, and for the first couple years, Dad would kind of expect him to come back."

Digger grimaced. "Very sad. But did he say what 'too much' meant."

"I guess they didn't call it PTSD in the early 1960s, but when I was a teenager, my grandmother said he was really depressed after the war. He was in D-Day. On the beach that first day."

"*Dang.*"

"He saw a lot of death. That must've been hard on him."

"Yeah, well it would be. After he and my grandmother married, he inherited his parents' dairy farm, and he liked to be in the pastures or do the milking, but my grandmother pretty much ran it. Before and after he vanished. She told me he was a good man, and he worked hard at whatever he did, but he wasn't himself after the war. Something like that."

"Nowadays most people don't say 'the' war. Too many to pick from."

As a history major, Digger agreed with him. But she didn't want to hear that just now. "So, Brian, what can I help you with?" She didn't add "that didn't take much time," but she didn't have it to give.

"I want you to show me how to look for people. You know, with genealogy."

"Because you think there's an outside chance he went elsewhere and he'll show up now?"

"Well, not *him*. He was born in 1915. But maybe he had kids somewhere else. They could be alive."

"Did you submit a DNA test to Ancestry or 123?"

Brian nodded. "About three or four weeks ago. I guess I should hear anytime. I want to get ready to look when I have that."

THE UNSCHEDULED MURDER TRIP

"Ah. Did you create a tree on Ancestry?"

"No, would that help?"

"You're going to have to start from square one."

Digger faced her computer and pulled the keyboard to her. "I'll show you how it works."

She switched her Internet browser to Ancestry.com. "I'll show you my tree and the messages I get from people who also sent in their DNA and think we're connected."

On Ancestry's home page, Digger selected the Browning and Muldoon family tree she had created.

"Who are the Muldoons?" Brian asked.

"My mom's maiden name." Digger went to her own name and pointed to the right of it, which showed her parents' names, with her and her sister under them. "Now watch." She clicked on her father and her paternal grandparents showed, with a list of all of their children.

"That looks like a lot of work."

She shrugged. "I didn't do it in a weekend. And you don't have to enter everyone from every family to get started." She turned toward him. "You have an Ancestry account, right? You needed it to do a DNA test." Digger logged out and slid her keyboard to him.

"What am I doing?" Brian asked.

"That's the question of the day."

"Sign into your Ancestry account, and I'll show you how to create a tree and enter a few names." She stood and stayed behind Brian, offering advice on entering his own information and that of his parents.

The phone rang.. Holly answered and gestured to Digger to take the call.

"Who is it?" Digger mouthed.

Holly gave her a brilliant smile.

She thought she knew what that meant. She reached for the desk phone. "Digger Browning here."

"Hey, Digger, it's Marty."

She liked the amiable reporter for the *Maple Grove News*, but he was more interested in dating than being friends. She'd told him she preferred the friends concept. He agreed, but his subtle hints continued.

"Hello. You working on a big story?" Digger, with her back to Brian, pointed a finger at Holly and mouthed, "You'll get yours."

"Always are. You want to meet for coffee?"

"There's your way to get rid of the kid."

Without thinking, Digger said, "What?"

Uncle Benjamin laughed.

Marty spoke louder. "You want to have a cup of coffee? I could meet you at the Coffee Engine."

"Gee, I'm…" She realized what Uncle Benjamin meant. "That could work, but can I bring you a story?"

WHEN SHE AND BRIAN arrived at the Coffee Engine, Marty sat at the large corner table, which, as usual, had X's taped at six-foot intervals. She and Brian pulled up their face masks and Marty did the same. Marty's eyes traveled to the papers Brian clutched and back to Digger.

"Good to see you," Digger said.

"Where's my seat?"

Marty stood and nodded. "I told the barista to put two more coffees on my tab." He reached out an arm to fist bump with Brian.

Digger introduced the men. "Brian is trying to track down his grandfather, who disappeared decades ago."

"Would that be Daniel Stevens?"

Brian's large brown eyes brightened. "Yes! Do you know someone who knew him?"

Marty sat again and smiled. "Grab the coffees for you and Digger, and come right back."

"Uh, sure." Brian hurried across the room.

"Are you trying to unload him?" Marty asked.

"You bet your ass she is."

"Not really. If you know his grandfather's story, you might like this update." She grinned. "I remember you wrote the last one."

"I do it every couple years. Because he went missing right after JFK was killed it's an easy date to remember."

Digger nodded. "He wants help with family tracing. He wonders if his grandfather started a second life somewhere."

Marty lowered his voice. "Even if he did, he'd be past 100. The odds of his being alive aren't good."

Brian balanced two cups of coffee as he walked toward them. Before he sat, he took sugar, artificial sweetener, and a few cream pods from his pocket and placed them on the table. "Didn't know how you like it."

"Cream, thanks." Brian sat and she continued, "I gave Marty a really brief summary of what you're doing."

Without touching his coffee, Brian opened the folded papers he left on the table. "Digger's showing me how creating a tree on Ancestry.com can help people find me through our DNA tests."

She slid her mask down to sip coffee and listened as Brian relayed events just before his grandfather vanished, and why he wanted to pursue the matter now.

Marty nodded as Brian talked, and when he finished, said, "I'm sorry about your father's illness. Does he, uh, know what you're doing?"

Digger hadn't thought to ask that.

Brian glanced away for a minute. "He knows how interested I am, and he's answered all my questions. I guess…well, it's been a long time. He gave up hoping long before I was born."

"I know you would love to find out something, but have you considered how easy it was back then to leave one place and start another life thousands of miles away?"

"Yes, no computers. Some workplaces didn't even ask for your Social Security number."

"True," Marty said. "And birth certificates didn't have fancy paper and watermarks like they do today. Might not have been hard for someone to forge one."

Brian's face fell, but he busied himself by putting cream and sugar in his coffee. "But the DNA stuff." He met Marty's skeptical expression. "My dad never did it, but he could have half-siblings he never knew about."

"I guess that's true. Have you thought about how that will affect a lot of lives if you do find someone?"

"I told you to ask that."

Brian sighed. "I'm not totally sure I'd try to meet them. Maybe sometime. Right now, I just want my dad to know."

"Baloney. You'd drive five hundred miles to see them."

For the thousandth time, Digger wished there were some sort of telepathy that would let her tell Uncle Benjamin to close his trap.

Marty tapped the table. "I'm a thorough reporter, so I have a file of clippings. And the newspaper got notes over the years."

Brian sat up straighter.

"None of them panned out. I don't know if a person was being mean when they sent information about a possible sighting, or they genuinely thought they saw him."

Brian interrupted. "But somebody checked it out, right?"

"My file has some handwritten notes about phone calls people made. They pretty much stopped checking after about ten years."

"Do you know who sent the notes?"

Marty shook his head. "I'm happy to show you what we've got, as long as you don't publicize anything that wasn't in the paper already."

Brian grinned broadly. "It's so great to be working with a team."

CHAPTER FIVE

BEFORE THEY LEFT THE Coffee Engine, Digger agreed to meet Marty for lunch the next day. Brian's project would give them something to talk about besides their own lives.

The short distance to her office passed the Chamber of Commerce, which had recently had the trim on all windows painted a deep green. Of all the narrow, two-story buildings on Main Street, it had the most formal appearance. The door jingled as she opened it.

"Hey, Digger, just like old times."

She grinned. "Abigail, you look as much at home as the office manager here as you did as my boss at the ad agency."

"And I love it. People in and out all day. I've learned about every business in town. Lots of good things happening."

"We could use a few more." Digger leaned on the counter that separated the reception area from Abigail's desk and a couple of others. "How many businesses shut because of COVID?"

"You probably know most of them. That art store, and the children's clothing place. Oh, and a few days ago, that new restaurant at the edge of town."

"Eats and Greets. I liked that place."

"Good burgers. You never know, some things get reincarnated."

"Only the best things."

Digger did a mental eye roll. "Do tell."

"Can't, sorry. Confidential discussions. What brings you in?"

"I took a bunch of pictures at the depot today. I'll go through them and bring you a flash drive with some of the best ones."

"Can you email them? I'll lose a flash drive."

"Files are too big. I can reduce the size of a couple and send them so you can resend them to other people, but you won't want to use those images for any publication."

"I know the Chamber Board will appreciate them. Did you notice if the electricity had been turned back on out there?"

"I feel silly. Didn't even try the switch. Why is it going to be back on?"

Abigail stapled the few pieces of paper she held. "They'll have tools to plug in when they start renovation."

"I saw the piles of roofing shingles outside. That gets to what I wanted to ask. I thought I'd take some pictures as they did the work. You could do a sort of collage and hang it out there. I know you're planning a display case with old mementos and maybe odd stuff unearthed during remodeling."

"We sure are."

"So, I don't want to drive out there every day. Will you hear about what's going on when?"

Abigail leaned on her side of the counter. "Since we're managing the renovations, I generally would. Can't promise I'll know exact days they're doing something, but close. In fact," she glanced toward a hallway behind her. "There's going to be some sort of ceremony out there next week, I think when some equipment they'll use for renovation arrives."

"Equipment?"

"Lots of water problems. Not sure what they're doing. They'll do a ribbon-cutting when it opens, but this will sort of announce the major repairs."

"Guess it'll be in Friday's paper," Digger said.

"Gene submitted the article yesterday. They'll probably edit it."

Digger tilted her head toward the hallway, where the chamber director had his office.

Abigail nodded.

"They do that. Remember the time...?"

Gene's bellow came from near enough that Digger realized he'd been listening. Good thing she hadn't asked about his recent effort to lose weight.

He appeared in the hallway entrance. "They butchered the piece we gave them on why we canceled the Fall Festival."

"Guess his diet isn't working."

Digger turned her snort into a cough as she pulled up her mask. "Excuse me. I did like that the article mentioned we'll have an even bigger parade next year."

Both of Gene's chins wiggled as he nodded. "Yes, but they took out the paragraphs with the history of the festival."

"You weren't writing for a tourist magazine."

Digger kept her expression neutral. "Sometimes they have to edit for space."

He didn't look mollified. "I suppose. I'm glad Abigail mentioned the thing at the depot next week. Can you come out to take pictures?"

Digger suppressed an expression of irritation, and smiled instead. She and Holly were walking a tightrope between what they should do for free or very reduced rates, in the hope of getting more business later. "Sure. Try to think about any group pictures you want. Folks don't wander around if they know they're going to be in one."

"Good idea." Gene turned to go back into his office.

Digger didn't want to be uncharitable, but the word waddle always came to mind when she watched Gene walk. Especially from behind.

HOLLY GREETED HER WITH a mild reproach. "If you've ditched the newbie family historian, let's get to work on the display ad for the downtown businesses."

"Sure. Sorry for the delay."

"No worries. I've done some initial layout; you can go through the photos you took last week to see what works."

Digger spent almost half-an-hour sorting through electronic files. She'd taken pictures of every business on Main Street and a few on side streets. Because the project was for the *Maple Grove News*, they would actually make a little money.

She settled on eleven pictures for the collage that would go in the middle of the full-page spread, and listed the photo numbers on a piece of paper so she and Holly could go over them on her screen. She stood and turned toward Holly and promptly dropped the paper with the list.

Uncle Benjamin stood in front of her, resplendent in an Uncle Sam costume, complete with top hat.

"Did you know this place has an attic? There's a bunch of costumes up there. Looks like they're used in the Fourth of July parade."

Digger had only seen her great uncle in the outfit he'd been buried in – his favorite red cardigan, a cream-colored button-down shirt, and bright green tie. He had worn the combination every Christmas, so she and Franklin had decided it would suit him.

She swore as she stooped to retrieve the paper. "Life is full of surprises."

"That's a big duh."

Holly looked up. "At least you didn't drop a cup of coffee."

"What? Oh, right. Easier to deal with paper than brown liquid."

Holly gave her one of those looks that seemed to say she thought her business partner was in an early stage of dementia. Which, since she talked to a ghost, maybe she was.

Digger sat the paper on the edge of Holly's desk. "These are in a folder called Newspaper Work on the shared drive. I'll pour myself some coffee while you have a first look." She turned to their kitchen corner and took a mug from the cabinet.

Digger put a coffee pod in the machine and pushed the brew button. Then she had a brainstorm. She picked up the small notepad on the counter – ideas could strike any time – and grabbed the pen affixed to the teabag canister with a line of yarn.

Quickly she wrote, "Now you can change clothes?"

"News to me. It's a good thing, too. There's some great stuff up there."

She scratched out the words she had written, put cream in her coffee and went to stand behind Holly. "When I was walking back just now, I looked up at our window and realized the building is much taller than this second floor. Do you suppose there's an attic?"

"Don't give away my secrets!"

"Never thought about it. Makes sense." She had moved eight pictures to a new folder she'd labeled Use These. "I liked the one of the variety store best, but they had so much Halloween stuff in the window you can see it. I think it would kind of timestamp the collage."

"I hadn't thought of that. Maybe we can have the jewelry store photo cover part of their display window."

They talked for another minute and Digger returned to her own computer to do a photo spread of the chosen pictures. When she looked up, Uncle Benjamin was sitting cross-legged on the right side of her desk. "Good God!"

"What? Are you okay?"

Digger swallowed. "I thought I had just lost the work. Pushed the Undo icon and it came back."

"Don't scare me like that, woman."

"Sorry. I'm going to have to learn how to bite my tongue. Got used to sitting in a cubicle alone."

Digger pulled a piece of discarded copy paper from the recycle shoebox on her desk and wrote. "You can't do stuff like that when I'm working. Go explore the attic some more."

"I'll take that as permission to do it the rest of the time."

The Uncle Sam character was gone as fast as he'd appeared.

CHAPTER SIX

DIGGER PLANNED TO SPEND the weekend getting the Ancestral Sanctuary ready for winter, including putting plastic on the interior of a lot of the windows. Windows from the early part of the twentieth century let in as much wind as a toddler playing with a screen door. She calculated that if she pinched pennies, each year she could buy at least one new window for the place, maybe two.

When she walked in the door at four-thirty Friday evening, Bitsy did not greet her with his usual urgency after being in the house alone all day. Because her cousin Franklin's car sat in the circular drive, she knew he'd let the German Shepherd outside already.

Digger scratched his head and entered the living room looking for his stuffed lamb. He had placed it on the table in front of the window, an odd choice for him. "Get your lamb, Bitsy. I want to go upstairs and check on Franklin's progress."

She could hear her cousin pounding something on the third floor, where he was turning part of the attic into a self-contained apartment for himself. At least he hoped Digger's high school friend, Cameron, would tell him he could run pipes up there from the second-floor bathroom. If not, it would be a fancy two-room suite, minus facilities.

Digger walked down the hall, through the living room, into the large, farmhouse-style kitchen and stopped. "Ragdoll, you know you aren't supposed to sit on the table!"

"She wanted to sit with me."

Digger picked up a napkin ring from the counter and threw it in the direction of Uncle Benjamin's voice and the cat. "Don't just pop up like that!"

"I've been sitting on this table with my cat for an hour. You're the one who just showed up."

That interested Digger. "She knows you're there?"

"Think so. She follows me from place to place, unless I get too high. Did you know there's a lot of dust on that ceiling fan in the dining room?"

"You should have cleaned it," Digger muttered.

"Your job now."

From the top of the back stairway came Franklin's voice. "I hope that's you, cuz. Who're you talking to?"

"Just trying to convince Ragdoll not to sit on the kitchen table."

"We may need to sprinkle water on her when she does stuff like that. I found her inside my toolbox this afternoon."

"I wanted to see if he had that set of screwdrivers I gave him when he bought his place in DC."

"I'm all for a gentle way to get her to behave." She lowered her voice to a whisper. "Wish it would work for some other people."

"You home for dinner tonight?" Franklin asked.

"Yep. How about if I do some homemade macaroni and cheese, and I think I have some broccoli."

"You definitely do. I brought a bunch of fresh vegetables and put them in the fridge."

"Thanks. Dinner'll be ready in about an hour and a half."

"Roger. Back to framing the new room." He walked through the upstairs hallway toward the stairway that led to the attic.

Digger turned toward the kitchen table and spoke quietly. "Did you stay home today because you knew Franklin was coming up?"

"Partly. I thought I'd give you and that reporter guy a chance to eat lunch alone."

"Thanks, but we don't discuss anything private."

As Digger turned to wash her hands at the sink, the napkin ring fell from the kitchen table to the floor. Ragdoll jumped down after it.

"I thought you hadn't been able to make anything move since you popped up that first day." The day of his burial, she'd almost wet herself when he appeared and announced that the minute they put the last shovel of dirt over his casket he'd found himself sitting on his and Aunt Clara's headstone.

"That was some kind of residual solid-being stuff. I'm trying to learn how to do it now that I'm clear-headed, so to speak."

"Swell. Do not try to surprise me by knocking more stuff off counters."

But Uncle Benjamin must have left, because he didn't answer. They had an agreement that he would respond if she called for him or asked a question. Otherwise, it would be too disconcerting to think someone was always in a room with her.

Digger finished scrubbing her hands and jogged up the main stairway in the front hall. She changed into lightweight jeans and a long-sleeved t-shirt that said, "I really dig cemeteries."

She put the mac and cheese together, with lots of shredded cheese and a dash of garlic salt added to the milk. As she put it in the oven, the phone rang.

"Digger Browning here."

"Hi, Digger. It's Brian Stevens."

"Hey, Brian. How's the hunt going?"

"Good and weird at the same time. I got my DNA results. I think my grandfather had at least some family I never even knew about."

"What did you find?"

He cleared his throat. "It linked me to several people, most of whom haven't shared their trees."

"So you can't tell if they're related to your mom's family or your dad's?"

"I've worked more on my family tree on Ancestry, but I haven't figured where people fit in."

"So what's your next step?"

"I expanded my online tree, and started with what I knew for sure. Then I've worked back. That meant starting with the 1940 census. Did you know it's on microfilm at the historical society?"

Digger thought that would take him forever. "That would be a huge amount of film to go through. If you have a subscription, you can use Ancestry's digital files. Easier to search."

"I started there, and found my grandfather and his parents. So then I went from 1940 to the 1930 census."

"You are getting into this."

"I feel like a detective. So, in 1930, I found what looked like a sister to my grandfather. I went to the microfilm because the online stuff was kind of muddy. I thought maybe the woman was a cousin and it got transcribed wrong. But she's on the 1930 census with my grandfather and his family. On the dairy farm. And," his voice rose, "she was a baby in 1930. She'd be about 90. She could be alive!"

Digger picked up a pencil and notepad. "It's…possible. What's her name?"

"Maryann Stevens. My grandfather was born in 1915, so he was twenty-five in 1940, but she's not there. Do you suppose she died?"

Though she thought that the most likely option as she jotted the name, Digger said, "The census counts everyone who was living in a household when the census taker visited. If a kid was at school, they're listed with their parents. If she visited relatives for a month, she could be in their household, or if she had TB or something, she'd be listed in a hospital."

"I'm going to find her. When my grandfather died in 1963, she would have been thirty-three. She must know something."

"Is she mentioned in his obituary as a surviving sibling?" Digger asked.

"No, it just lists my grandmother, my dad, and his sister Carol."

"Did you ask your dad about his father having a sister?" She figured Matthew Stevens would know if he had an aunt, even if she wasn't around.

"I will, but I wanted to ask if you had any more places I could look."

Digger envisioned an earnest expression on his eager face. "Are you in front of your computer?"

"Yep. My laptop."

"Okay. Go back to…did you say her name?"

"Maryann Stevens, born about 1930. I can get back to her name on the census."

"Did you add her to your grandfather's family as his sibling? If you didn't, do it real fast. I'll stay on the line. I'm going to do a couple quick things and I'll be back to the phone."

She took lettuce, carrots, and broccoli out of the refrigerator and placed them in one side of the double sink to wash. She dug in the silverware drawer and found the carrot peeler before she picked up the phone again. "Brian?"

"Yes, I added her. I'm in her record."

"So, go back to the 1930 census and associate her record with the child on the 1930 census. Then we'll see if more information pops up."

Digger could hear him typing. She wanted to tell him to call back later, but he was in the genealogy zone. When she first started family history research, every new find was as good as getting a bonus at work.

Brian was back in two minutes. "When I connected her to my grandfather's family, a couple things did show. She didn't die, well, not young, anyway. There's a picture of her in a Frostburg elementary school yearbook. As a teacher."

"What year?"

"Um. The school's 1955 yearbook."

"So, she's pretty young. After you link that to her, more things should pop up."

"Okay, doing that." More typing. "I wish we could get the 1950 census data."

"So does every other family historian in the country. Should be 2023 or thereabouts."

"Huh. Nothing else comes up as a hint. Does it usually take this long?"

Digger laughed.

"What?"

She laughed harder, and finally took a breath. "I'm sorry, Brian. It struck me so funny. You're used to immediate response from the Internet. I can still see Uncle Benjamin on the floor of the courthouse in Oakland, looking toward the very back of this deep shelf to see if pages from the first marriage book for Garrett County had fallen back there."

"Oh, right. Not on the Internet."

"No, no Internet. Just for fun, when you have some time off, ask Thelma Zorn at the historical society to talk to you about how they developed indexes for all the county census records for Maple Grove by going to the National Archives and taking notes."

"Uh, okay."

Digger realized she didn't know something. "I forgot to ask, what do you do for a living?"

"I'm a senior in college. Our lectures are via remote learning, so I'm home."

"That's a bummer."

His tone was matter-of-fact. "I can use the library over at Frostburg University, and I get to spend time with my dad."

"Sure. What's the other thing you found?"

"One of those phone book references. From about the same time, in Frostburg."

"I have to get something out of the oven."

"Oh, sorry."

"No problem. Look for marriage records, since she would probably have changed her name back then, and consider that she may have moved out of the area."

They hung up, and Digger figured Brian would have a lot more luck if his aunt had a five-syllable name or a profession other than teaching. She'd once found a distant cousin because she was a junior scientist on the Sabin team that developed the oral polio vaccine.

Franklin's footsteps headed down the back stairs toward the kitchen. "Hey, cuz. Something smells good."

Uncle Benjamin sniffed, but from his look of disappointment, he didn't smell anything.

"That's because you don't have a very discerning palette. I'm great at macaroni and cheese and pot roast."

Franklin tugged the long braid that fell below Digger's shoulders. "Don't put yourself down."

"That's my boy."

"Deal. You want to take the Pyrex pan out of the oven and set it on top of the stove?"

"Sure. Who were you talking to?"

Digger began washing the broccoli. "Long story. If you get bored, you can stop me in the middle."

AN HOUR LATER, DIGGER and Franklin began what had become an after-dinner ritual – even after dark -- a walk from the Ancestral Sanctuary's front porch down the long drive. When they got the eighth-of-a-mile to the road, they turned and walked back.

Franklin had suggested that walk when he got home the morning after Digger found Uncle Benjamin's body at the bottom of the cellar stairs. It had a calming effect then, and Digger looked forward to their talks as they walked.

Franklin was twelve years older than she, and they had not lived in the same house. They didn't now, but he came west from his home on Dupont Circle in DC at least twice a month, usually for a three-day weekend. Ostensibly, he came to work on the apartment he had designed for the attic, but Digger knew it was as much to be sure she was okay. You didn't find a body just any old day.

Franklin nodded toward the 100-year-old house, the third built on that spot. "You've done a lot to make the place homey again. Do you ever regret he left it to you?"

For a second, Digger wondered if the question was a back-door way to say he was still hurt that his father left the four-acre mountain property to his niece instead of his son. She must have stiffened.

Franklin laughed softly. "You know I got over it fast. I did get the money." He nudged her elbow.

She nudged him back. "I know. That's why I'm letting you spend some of it to build out the attic."

Bitsy barked and came running toward them from the back of the house. "He's mad we didn't take him for the walk."

"He was snoozing on the back porch."

Digger nodded toward the front of the house, where a window showed Ragdoll sitting on a table, bathed in light from a ginger-jar lamp. "I've given up trying to keep her off that table."

"Dad always let her sit there. Called her his guard cat." He stooped to scratch Bitsy's head and he fell into step beside them.

"To answer your question, I don't regret getting the place. I'm not sure I can keep it forever."

"What the hell? It has to stay in the family."

"You miss being in town?"

Digger nodded. "Sometimes, but more often I like the silence out here." She tilted her head toward the Gardiner home. "Neighbors a quarter mile away and all that."

"So why leave?"

"I can haunt you wherever you go."

Digger stumbled for a second on a large piece of gravel. "Clumsy. I could see living here if I got married…"

Franklin elbowed her.

"You're as bad as Holly. Marty Hofstedder and I are just friends."

"Uh huh."

Digger ignored the humor in his tone. "But kids. You grew up here. Wasn't it lonely?"

Franklin sighed. "Especially after Mom died. She and I went into town together a lot."

Digger expected a comment from Uncle Benjamin, but none came. "Anyway, it could work to stay here, but I'd have to think about it."

"Speaking of kids, I've been thinking about the Stevens kid. His name's Brian?"

"Yep. He's not a kid, he's twenty-two."

"You're pushing your late twenties and I still call you kid. Does he understand that finding unknown relatives he could be ruffling some feathers?"

"Marty mentioned that to him in the Coffee Engine on Thursday."

Franklin grinned. "Ah, the ubiquitous Marty."

"Stop already."

"You better quit leading that guy on. Reporters know how to dig, too."

"I'm not…oh, you. Friends, that's it."

"Famous last words. I've been thinking about who his father, Matthew, is. Wasn't he a firefighter in town? One of the two paid ones?"

"Gee, I never asked what his dad did, we only talked about him having cancer."

"If he's who I think he is, he knew, knows, half the town. Seems as if he would have had a lot of people to talk to about his father, a lot of people to question if he wanted to look into it more."

"His father is the most stand-offish firefighter I ever met."

Digger started and almost stumbled into Franklin.

Franklin touched her elbow. "Been nipping the cooking sherry, cuz?"

"Tell him how you took a nip the first time you saw me."

"Nope. Just a klutz. That's a good point. Brian kind of dodged my question when I asked if his dad approved. Just said he'd answered any questions Brian had."

"You know the expression. Sometimes it's best to let sleeping dogs lie."

CHAPTER SEVEN

SUNDAY MORNING BROUGHT BRILLIANT sunshine and cold weather. Digger hoped it would warm up late in the week, before the ribbon cutting at the train depot.

Brian called in the late afternoon, and he only had to say hello for Digger to hear the emotion in his voice.

"What is it?"

"I found Maryann Stevens, but my father is really angry with me."

Digger glanced at Bitsy, asleep on his dog bed in front of the fireplace in the living room. "Did he already know where she was?"

"Not exactly, but he knew who she was. She married a man named Montgomery, and they moved to Ohio for a time. They came back to the county and her husband had an insurance agency in Oakland."

A bell dinged in the back of Digger's brain. "So, her children would be your dad's first cousins."

"Yes, but they never socialized or anything. I guess Grandfather Daniel's sister was convinced he would never have left his wife and two kids, and my grandmother, Isabella, eventually accepted that he did."

"And that caused a rift?"

"So much so that when Maryann wanted my grandmother to meet her oldest child, she said no."

"Wow. I'm sorry, Brian. When did Maryann die?"

"She didn't. She's in a retirement home in Oakland. I don't know what her faculties are. But I found out I'm second cousins to Sheriff Roger Montgomery."

When she heard the name Montgomery, Digger had thought of that possibility. It meant Brian was connected to a powerful

Garrett County family, whether he knew that yet or not. Sheriff Montgomery's ancestors were some of the original county settlers in the late 1700s or early 1800s. They owned substantial tracts of land close to the county seat. And they gave regularly to politicians in the area.

Some said that Sheriff Montgomery's election to that post had been a done deal when he ran the first time, but Digger didn't know that to be true. And what if it were? He was a good sheriff, and he helped her a lot when Uncle Benjamin died. "Have you met the sheriff?"

"I know who he is, of course. The sheriff works out of Oakland, right?"

"There's a small office in the basement of our city hall, so they don't have to drive across the mountains as much. He's there a lot."

"You think I should go meet him?" Brian asked.

"Maybe first tell me why your dad is upset."

"Mostly I think he doesn't want to deal with any of it. Like me meeting Maryann Stevens…Montgomery's family."

Digger had a feeling that Matthew Stevens and Roger Montgomery very well knew they were related, even if they didn't acknowledge it to each other. She thought for a moment. "You said you wanted to see if you could locate a second family for Daniel Stevens so you could let your father know what happened. It sounds as if he wants you to leave it alone. Are you willing to do that?"

After several seconds of silence, he said, "I'm not going to talk to him about it anymore. Unless I learn something concrete. He, well, he has probably a year to live."

"I'm sorry it's such a short time. But I think your decision makes sense."

"I still might see if I can meet Maryann Montgomery. I mean, she's ninety. Who knows if she'll be around in six months?"

"He's like a dog with a bone."

Digger ignored Uncle Benjamin. "Are any of Maryann Montgomery's children alive? Like Sheriff Montgomery's father?"

"I'm going to look into that."

"Perhaps do it quietly. Your dad and his cousin, or maybe cousins, could have reached out to each other over the years, and they didn't. For whatever reason."

"Yeah, I guess."

"It's not up to me to tell you what to do, but maybe some of those Montgomery cousins will have submitted their DNA, and you'll come across them later. That would give you a sort of neutral reason to contact them."

"Good idea. Plus, I have a lot of studying to do the next few days. Even when you're remote, you have exams."

As Digger finished the call, Franklin came down the hallway staircase. He planned to return to DC earlier than usual, because he had to prepare a response for some client's lawsuit. She knew little about his work, and he discussed it rarely.

He set a backpack on the dining room table. "Okay, cuz, you have a busy week ahead of you?"

"Not too bad. Meeting with a couple businesses to try to get them to let us do short marketing videos they can run on local TV."

"You know how to do that?"

"It's so simple these days, even your father could have learned it."

"That technology gets simpler all the time."

"That's insulting."

Digger kept herself from laughing. "And there's a ceremony of some sort before they start renovating the train depot to be a visitor center. I'll take some photos."

"For a fee?" he asked.

"We'll figure out a way to sell some of the photos eventually."

Franklin offered Digger an elbow. "I can't wait for this COVID crap to be over."

She elbow-bumped him and smiled. "Gotten worse up here. Can't wait for the vaccine. Then I can come visit you."

"Good. Don't undervalue yourself."

Digger walked him to the front porch.

"Tell him to drive slow down the mountain."

"Enjoy driving that Volvo down the mountain."

"That's not what I said."

"Always do."

Digger waved good-bye as Franklin pulled away. "Wherever you are, it would be really weird for me to tell him that on a nice day."

"I suppose. He drives too fast. Don't want him out there in the plot with his mother and me."

"Franklin can take care of himself. I'm going to make a cup of tea and I want you to tell me more about this Stevens-Montgomery connection."

"I have stuff to do first. I'll meet you in the kitchen in a couple hours."

DIGGER STOOD IN THE kitchen two hours later. "Uncle Benjamin?"

No response.

She started the tea kettle, put a teabag in a mug, and tried again, "Are you here?"

When Uncle Benjamin didn't respond, she muttered, "Would be nice if you'd let me know where you are in the house."

"Sorry. Had to do some research."

Digger took in Uncle Benjamin's clothes, and gasped. "That's the suit you used to wear to other people's funerals."

"Yeah. I figured out that I can imagine myself wearing whatever I want, so I did. And there I was, looking in the mirror with my best shirt and tie."

"That's creepy."

"Kinda fun. Plus, I'd only worn this suit a few times. It's got a lot of wear left."

Digger didn't want to spend time on her uncle's wardrobe choices. "We need some kind of system. If I have no clue where you are, it feels as if you could be looking over my shoulder all day."

"Maybe I am."

"I could move, you know. What would you do then?"

"You'd miss me."

"Like a mosquito on a summer night."

"What if I holler at you from the next room before I get close?"

"It's a start." She poured her tea. "Can you smell things?"

"So far, no. I keep putting my face over pots and pans when you cook. Nothing. You should try some of the recipes in your Aunt Clara's recipe box."

The box sat on the top shelf of the pantry, near the back stairs. "I'd have to buy a lot of Crisco. So will you always be the way you are now?"

"This gig doesn't come with an instruction manual. Are you insulting your aunt?"

"No. Cooking ingredients have changed. Less fat and salt now." She smiled. "I'm going to sit with my cup of tea and listen while you tell me what you know about Daniel Stevens."

"Not sure there's a lot to tell. I just went through my county family files. Thought I'd saved some articles, only found one."

"If it's been in the paper, I can find it. What gossip did you hear around town?"

"I never gossiped. But I did hear things in my hardware store."

When Uncle Benjamin and Aunt Clara owned it, the store had been a hub of local news. In part it was because of the free coffee. "And...?"

Ragdoll meowed and Uncle Benjamin patted a spot next to him on the red tabletop. *"Never occurred to me to sit up here when I was alive, and now it's my favorite spot."*

The cat jumped on a chair and then sat on the table, but she didn't react when Uncle Benjamin petted her.

"You were saying."

"I didn't know him or his wife well. They were more than fifteen years older, and they lived in the country."

"On his parents' dairy farm."

"Which he inherited. And that might explain some of the bad feelings between Isabella Stevens and his sister, Maryann, after Daniel died."

"How so?"

"I guess Daniel and Maryann's parents were old-fashioned. They left the farm only to him. I heard they left her a small amount of money, but it wasn't close to the value of the farm."

"So the rift between the families started when Daniel was alive?"

"Not so anybody saw. When he was alive, Daniel gave his sister a portion of the farm's profits every year. Wasn't a lot, but he thought it was fair, and she appreciated it."

"And Isabella stopped that?"

"I heard Maryann talking in the store one time, to Thelma Zorn."

"So Maryann resented Isabella?"

"Maryann understood. Isabella had the farm to run, the kids to raise, and she lost Daniel's income."

"He had a job before the quarry?"

"Besides the farm, his obit said he was a substitute mail carrier for a while. Then he and Harlan Jones bought the quarry and built up that business a fair amount."

"What did Maryann tell Thelma?"

"Somehow, Thelma had spotted the strain. Maryann said Isabella might've felt bad about not continuing the annual gift, and seeing Maryann reminded her of that."

"If she felt bad, she could have started up again."

Uncle Benjamin shrugged. *"I expect she didn't have anything extra."*

"So that's all you know?"

"Keep your shirt on. The big issue was that Maryann didn't think Daniel would have run away, and Isabella came to think he did. Guess he had some problems with depression after the War."

"So why cut off all contact? She was the kids' aunt. Matthew's aunt. Wait, who else was there?"

"A sister to Matthew. She moved to Colorado or somewhere for college and almost never came back. Her name'll come to me."

"Brian said her name is Carol Did she…?"

"Are you gonna let me finish?"

"Sure. Sorry."

"Not much more. The quarry was a smaller business then, so when Isabella decided she didn't want to run it with Jones, she got a little money, nothing like she would now."

"That's too bad."

"Maryann, she was closer to my age, was plain hurt when Isabella didn't want their kids to know each other. I think that

might've even been why she and her husband moved away. Don't know that."

Digger picked up her empty mug and carried it to the sink. "Kind of sounds as if Brian may have found all there is to know about relatives."

CHAPTER EIGHT

DIGGER PUT BRIAN STEVENS out of her mind the next two days. Despite what she'd told Franklin about making short videos being fairly simple, it had to be done just right or the television spots would look like amateur You-Tube pieces. She placed Bitsy in several locations in the house and tried filming her with different lighting.

"You know where I'd like to go?"

"Damn it, Uncle Benjamin, you said you'd let me know before you come into a room."

"I get bored hanging around here and following your day at work."

"I get tired of being so startled I jump a foot."

"You know, there's lot of ghost towns along the Potomac River, on the Maryland and West Virginia sides."

"Mostly old coal company towns."

"Right. You think anyone lives there?"

"No, some of them are barely piles of rubble, the companies left and the people…oh. You mean are there…people like you?"

"Maybe. I'd like to check 'em out."

Digger found the idea intriguing, but if she ended up being able to see other ghosts, she'd probably need to check herself into some sort of mental health facility. "Have you seen other spirits?"

"Not a one. Not even in our little cemetery. Keep looking for Clara."

She hadn't considered that Uncle Benjamin felt lonely. "You looking for company?"

"Maybe. I mostly want to see if they're like me."

"Ornery and obstreperous?"

"Charming and debonair. You want to visit some of them?"

45

She sighed. Visiting ghost towns in cold weather would not be at the top of any tourist's list and certainly wasn't on hers. "I have a busy couple of weeks. Can it wait?"

"I 'spose. You seeing that Marty fellow?"

"Just around town. Speaking of which, I'm heading there. Are you coming with me?"

"I want to explore the attic of your building. There's lots more than trunks of old costumes."

HOLLY AND DIGGER FINISHED designing a brochure for the Maple Grove Bank and Trust when the phone rang. "I'd like to hear that jingle more often," Holly said.

Digger nodded and picked up the land-line phone. "You Think, We Design."

"Marty Hofstedder here. Want to take a drive to the old depot?"

"I thought that ribbon cutting thing was Thursday." She held the phone away from her ear so Holly could hear.

"It is, but they're taking out that old sundial. Could be a good photo op for your historical society stuff."

"Could be. I didn't see any announcement."

"Hasn't been one. Since the Chamber bought the property, they can do what they want, but they don't want a bunch of what your friend Abigail calls history nuts protesting."

"How about if Holly and I meet you out there?"

Holly pointed a finger at her and shook her head.

"Oh, uh, sure. I saw those guys who dig graves for the cemetery heading that way a couple minutes ago. They had a small bulldozer on a flatbed and one of them was driving the yellow front-end loader."

Digger's stomach clenched. Don Phelps and a man named Stan – she couldn't remember his last name, or if she'd ever known it -- had come to the Ancestral Sanctuary to dig Uncle Benjamin's grave. She hadn't seen them since. "I'll leave now and meet you out there." She hung up.

"You really should at least go to the movies in Frostburg with him."

"I keep telling you he won't give up."

46

Digger ignored both comments and told Holly she'd probably be back in less than an hour.

The morning frost had burned off early, but she could still see her breath. When she pulled onto the gravel near the depot, Digger put on gloves and a knit cap. She'd have to take off the gloves to take the pictures, but her hands didn't have to be icicles all the time.

Marty stood next to the belching truck that held a small bulldozer. The front-end loader sat closer to the road. At least Don and Stan didn't have the backhoe they used to dig graves. She knew they used a front-end loader to move heavy headstones from one spot to another. They probably needed it to move the sundial.

A couple long strands of some sort of canvas belt hung on the side panel of the truck. The two men were placing long metal strips on the back of the flatbed truck so they could drive the small bulldozer off.

"Seems like a lot of work when they could just knock the damn thing over."

Digger waved to Marty and he started toward her. She pretended to rub her nose. "You're supposed to value history."

"Bet that old sundial weighs five hundred pounds."

Marty gestured behind him. "I heard that thing was a tourist attraction of sorts, but I guess it's not worth it to replace the dial someone ripped off."

"I heard that. I saw Leon Jones out here the other day, and he said there used to be a small garden surrounding it."

They walked toward the depot. "Huh. I'll have to see if I can find an old picture with the garden, run it next to the ones of these guys taking it out."

Digger suddenly remembered she hadn't returned the key to the padlock. She supposed Abigail knew it was safe with her, but she needed to take it back to the Chamber. "I can let us in if you want to look around. Abigail said they turned the electricity back on."

"Bet that's some old wiring."

"You looking for a story about an electrical fire?"

"That joke'll make an audience wipe tears from their eyes."

"Not a fan of covering fires."

Digger led them into the depot and Marty stared around the place. "Looked a lot bigger when the historical society had their shelves and tables in here."

They ambled around the building for a few minutes until the sound of the dozer reached them. "Time for a photo shoot," Marty said.

Digger had work boots, but she wished she'd thought to put on the better-insulated pair she had in the back of her Jeep. Walking on the cold ground soon had her so chilled she had to steady her arm by pressing her elbow to her side. If she didn't, the camera shook.

Don and Stan had tied sturdy pieces of canvas belt around the base of the sundial. Stan slowly moved the truck forward to pull on the sundial as Don shouted something unintelligible to him.

Digger shot from one angle, careful to stay out of Marty's line of sight so she didn't end up in his pictures.

After less than a minute of gentle tugging, the sundial tilted toward the dozer.

"Wonder where they're taking that old thing? Not like you can put it in a dumpster."

"Maybe the county landfill."

Marty cupped a hand around one ear and Digger waved and shook her head.

"You should tell him about me."

She turned so Marty couldn't see her mouth. "Like anyone would believe me."

"If you're going to spend more time with him, it'd be easier if we could all talk. I mean, you could tell him what I said."

"Or I could not tell him, and you wouldn't be involved in the conversations."

"That's no fun. I bet he knows what's going on all over town."

Finally, the sundial was fully loosened. Don drove the front-end loader over to angle the sundial onto its loading platform and moved it onto the flatbed truck.

She and Marty stood almost shoulder to shoulder. "Any bets on whether it falls into more than two pieces when they try to load it?"

"I'm in for four."

"I'd be surprised if it didn't. They put it there in the mid-sixties, I think," Marty said.

As the sundial, still in one piece, was loaded, Digger and Marty took a few pictures. "I want to get one of the hole that's left," Digger said.

"It's all yours. I'm turning on the heater in my car. Want to get a cup at the Coffee Engine?"

"I could do with some hot chocolate." Digger trudged to the spot where the sundial had been. Though the ground hadn't frozen as solid as it soon would, the cold meant the mix of mud and gravel was firm enough that she didn't sink into it.

As she snapped, Digger saw a bigger piece of the red material she'd picked up the other day. She stooped to retrieve it and found the earth clinging to it. She tugged, expecting it to pull up, but it didn't.

"Must be a big piece of carpet or whatever."

Digger tugged harder. The roughly four by five-inch piece of disintegrating carpet finally loosened. So did the bony finger beneath it.

DIGGER SAT IN MARTY'S car, appreciating its heater and watching Sheriff Montgomery and two deputies talk to the county medical examiner, Alex Cluster. She'd met the man briefly when he came to the Ancestral Sanctuary the night Uncle Benjamin died. He had the personality of a popsicle, but she supposed in his business there weren't a lot of hopeful days.

The car door opened and Marty rejoined her. "They're about to pull back just enough of the carpet to see if there's any ID or other identifying items. Sheriff told me to stay away and not take pictures."

"Ask him what the devil he saw."

"Did Sheriff Montgomery have any thoughts on how old that carpet was?"

"He and Dr. Cluster are talking about it. It's barely holding together, so they seem to think it was put there not too long after Daniel died, in the mid-sixties."

"Long time ago," Digger said.

"Brilliant observation."

"You thinking what I'm thinking?"

Digger nodded. "Unless some gangster came down from Pittsburgh or someplace, I can only think of one local missing person that fits that timeframe."

"Yep."

The men had their backs to Digger and Marty now, probably so they couldn't watch what the deputies did. All she could see was backsides and arms pointing down.

After about two minutes, Sheriff Montgomery nodded to the others and turned toward Digger and Marty. As he walked, the medical examiner's van pulled in perhaps twenty-five feet from them. He stopped to talk to the driver, deputy ME Penelope Parker, then jerked a thumb toward Cluster and walked toward Marty's car. He put the window down.

"You two doing okay?" He looked at Digger as he said it.

"Better," Digger said. "Never expected to see another dead person outside of a funeral home."

Montgomery nodded. "Rough year." He focused more on Marty. "I know all about the free press in this country, but I'd like you to not put too many details on your web page for a day or so. We'll have a better idea of what's going on in time for your Friday print edition."

Marty nodded. "Later this afternoon I can do a short piece about something being unearthed and say you're investigating, but by tomorrow I have to say more. If only because a couple deputies in your department talk to people at the Pittsburgh and Morgantown papers. I don't want to get scooped."

Montgomery grunted.

Digger leaned in front of Marty and met the sheriff's eyes. "Is it Daniel Stevens?"

"What in the hell made you guess that?" he asked.

"Tell him he's about to meet a first cousin once removed."

CHAPTER NINE

DIGGER LOOKED AWAY FOR a minute and then met Sheriff Montgomery's eyes again. "A few days ago, a young man named Brian Stevens contacted me. He wanted to know how to find out if his grandfather, who vanished in 1963, had appeared somewhere else, maybe had a second family."

"That Matthew's kid?"

Marty sat up straighter. "You knew about your cousins?"

"Crud. You digging into this? It's old news."

Digger noticed Sheriff Montgomery did not answer the question.

"It was, until just now. In fact, when Digger and I had coffee with Brian last week, we kind of gently said you never know what you'll turn up if you get into something like that."

"We sure didn't think it would be you," Digger added.

Montgomery turned to walk back to the depot. "You two can leave. We've asked you all I can think of for now. Don't call Matthew just yet. Or Brian. I need to tell Matthew in person."

Marty put up the window. To Digger, he said, "We try never to contact victims' families before the police or sheriff, but as soon as I see a deputy's car pull away from the Stevens' house, I want to call Brian. You have his number, right?"

"You're going to stake out their house?"

He half-shrugged. "Kind of. I looked it up. I can sit on a cross street near it."

Digger nodded slowly. "I feel so bad for Brian, and his dad. In a way…"

"It might have been better if Daniel were found after Matthew died?"

"Yes, if it upsets him. At least he'll know his father didn't desert the family."

"If Brian calls, will you contact me? Or ask him to?"
"I will unless he specifically asks me not to."

HOLLY LOOKED UP WHEN Digger returned to the office. She stood. "My God, Digger, what happened to you?"

"I, what? I'm fine. Well, I'm not, but I'm okay."

Holly gestured that Digger should walk closer. "You're pale and you look…frazzled. You need a hug."

Digger held up a hand. "Thank you, but you know…."

"Oh, right." Holly blew her a kiss.

Digger sat at the desk that faced Holly and pointed to Holly's chair. "It's a good thing you didn't come out to the depot."

"Ohmygod. Marty proposed and you told him no."

Digger put her chin on her chest for a moment. She raised her head. "No."

As she relayed finding Daniel's body, Holly's eyes slowly filled with tears. "That poor boy. I think he wanted good news."

"He did. He called over the weekend to say he had what could have been good news. He may have found more relatives. I mean, obviously not other descendants of his grandfather." Digger didn't want to have a long discussion about the Stevens-Montgomery estrangement, so she didn't say exactly who he found.

Just then, Uncle Benjamin came through the door, literally. He was more translucent than usual, and his hair was mussed. Digger would have described his expression as frantic.

"You left me! How could you leave me?"

Holly's voice cut through. "Digger, are you okay?"

She stood, "Sorry, quick bathroom break." She hurried down the hall and entered the single-stall restroom.

When Uncle Benjamin didn't follow, she gestured to him. When he came in, she shut the door and whispered. "Where were you? Weren't you in the car when I drove back?"

He leaned heavily on the basin and choked out a sob. *"You wanted me gone."*

It hit Digger that he must have been next to the sheriff deputies when she and Marty left. She reached out a hand and touched what looked to be his shoulder. "I'm sorry. I thought you were being quiet because it was so serious."

Uncle Benjamin straightened and held his hand at arm's length. *"Am I coming back?"*

"What do you mean?"

"When I followed you into town, I could see I kept getting paler. I think if it had been much farther I would have poofed out."

She smiled briefly. "I learned a new verb."

"It's not funny!"

"Of course…"

"Digger, are you okay?" Holly's tone was close to tremulous.

"I am. I'll be out in a minute."

Holly walked back toward their office, so she whispered, "Listen, I'm really sorry."

But Uncle Benjamin had disappeared.

FOR THE NEXT FEW HOURS, Digger listened for the phone and watched for her uncle. Had his spirit, or whatever he was, truly vanished? She thought of how she had scolded him for surprising her and wished she hadn't.

At two o'clock, Sheriff Montgomery called. "Digger, before we talk about what you found this morning, could you tell me how you hooked up with the Stevens family?"

"Sure. I didn't know them, but Brian, Matthew's son, knew I paid attention to local history, and he saw the article in the paper about Holly and me opening our business. He left me a note, initially, asking for advice on how to do some research."

Holly drew a question mark in the air, and Digger mouthed the sheriff's name.

"He specifically asked about Daniel Stevens?"

"Not in the note. Brian stopped by later, and I showed him how to create a tree on Ancestry.com. When he did that, he got to census records that showed his grandfather had a sister."

"And that led you to me?"

"Didn't lead me anywhere, Sheriff. He eventually figured out that the baby he saw on the 1930 census was Maryann Stevens

Montgomery." Digger stopped. She didn't mind telling the sheriff anything she could, but thought Brian should tell his own story.

"And he told you this?"

"Yes. Just this morning. Then Marty called to say they were taking down the sundial, and I met him out there to take some pictures."

"You working for the paper now?"

Irritation crept into her voice. "I think you know I'm not. I took pictures that we might use for business purposes. Maybe the Maple Grove Historical Society will do a report about the renovations at the depot."

Sheriff Montgomery let out an honest-to-goodness sigh. "I let Matthew and his family know we found what we believe to be the remains of Daniel Stevens. I also told Brian he can do any research on his own or with you, as long as he isn't interfering with any investigation I'm doing."

"You think you'll find a killer after all this time?"

"Hard to say."

"Don't you think the body had to be put there when the sundial was installed?"

"I make no assumptions when starting an investigation. Goodbye, Digger."

She hung up and looked at Holly. "You could hear a lot of that, right?"

Holly nodded. "That poor man died in what, 1963? Close to sixty years ago. Almost anyone who knew anything has to be dead."

"Agreed. I'm sorry Daniel Stevens' story had to end this way. I hope Brian leaves it alone."

"What more could he do? Personally, I mean."

Digger shrugged. "As far as the murder, I would think nothing. I hope he lets the issue about past family…disagreements stay in the past."

"Disagreements?"

Footsteps trudged up the staircase.

Digger quickly crossed the room and sat at her computer. "I'm officially busy."

"Damn straight you are," Holly said.

Someone knocked and the door opened. Brian came in, shut the door behind him, nodded at Holly, and turned to Digger. "I'm sorry you had to find him."

Digger gestured to a chair next to her desk. "Have a seat. I can take a break for a few minutes." She pulled up a Word document, not even sure of the topic.

When she didn't say anything, Brian did. "My dad took it pretty hard."

"I bet he did."

"Sure sorry to hear, Brian," Holly said.

"Thanks." He smiled in her direction and turned back to Digger. "He said as an adult, he always figured his father had to be dead. Now he wishes he hadn't been so angry at him when he was a kid."

"I'd have been resentful if one of my parents disappeared. Worried, too, but given the circumstances, you could see why your father and his mother could have thought he up and left."

He stood. "I have to get home. I came out to get some ginger ale for my dad. The cancer makes his stomach upset. I just wanted to be sure you're okay."

"That was good of you," Digger said.

As he walked out, she glanced around the room. Where could Uncle Benjamin be hiding? Maybe in the attic?

"Poor guy," Holly said. "At least his father won't have to wonder."

"It'll be front page news."

"What did you mean disagreements?"

"It seems Matthew's mother and Daniel's sister were estranged," Digger said.

"How do you know that?"

Digger hesitated. She had to remember what she heard from Uncle Benjamin and what Brian had said. "When Brian started hunting online, he found out about the sister, who would be his dad's aunt. He'd never heard of her. I don't know all the details."

Holly shook her head. "Not the time to remember the bad stuff."

"Agreed."

THE UNSCHEDULED MURDER TRIP

From behind her, Uncle Benjamin said, *"There'll be rumors galore. I bet it was that fellow he had the quarry with. It's always about money."*

Digger turned toward her computer, but glanced to her left as she did so. Uncle Benjamin sat atop the small photocopier, wearing a Daniel Boone-style hat and an imitation brown leather jacket like frontier men wore.

She pulled her computer toward her and picked up her notebook, as if consulting it before typing. "Are you okay?"

"Finally feeling better. Took a nap in one of the trunks. There's a lot of spiders up there."

She wanted to ask why spiders would bother a ghost, but didn't. Holly had moved to the drafting table near the window, so her back was to Digger. She opened a new document and typed, "I'll try to remember to look for you before I drive off."

"You can make it up to me by visiting one of the old ghost towns."

CHAPTER TEN

WHEN SHE GOT HOME, Digger walked Bitsy and fed both pets before calling Franklin to tell him she'd found Daniel Stevens.

"That's horrible. Do you need me to come up there?"

One reason Franklin had such a busy schedule in DC was because he wanted to be in Maple Grove a couple of times a month. Much more than before Uncle Benjamin died. "I'm okay. In a way, it brings closure to a lot of people, so it's not like finding your dad."

"No kidding. If you're okay, I'll stay here. Kiss Ragdoll for me."

Franklin hung up before Digger could tell him she wouldn't do it on a bet. The very fluffy cat left remnants of her fur all over the house, something Digger had a hard time getting used to. She'd taken to closing the upstairs doors so Ragdoll couldn't sleep in every room. Still, despite a cat bed in the corner of Digger's room, the cat ended up on her bed every night.

The phone rang as she put a frozen dinner in the microwave. Chicken Kiev, one of her favorites. "Digger Browning here."

After a second or two of silence, a soft woman's voice said, "I was calling for Beth Browning."

"Beth is my given name. Digger is a nickname, and I generally go by it. Can I help you?"

"I always did like Beth, but you liked Digger so much I adapted."

She jumped and scowled at the cross-legged figure on the kitchen table.

"My name is Nellie Porter. I live in the senior residence in Oakland, the Quiet Spring."

That had Digger's attention. Maryann Montgomery likely lived there. "Hello Ms. Porter. What can I do for you?"

"Years ago, almost sixty now, I worked at Mountain Granite Quarry, for Mr. Jones and Mr. Stevens."

THE UNSCHEDULED MURDER TRIP

Digger envisioned a thin, prim woman of at least eighty, perhaps sitting at the kind of writing desk well-to-do women might have used in the 1940s. "Oh. Did you, uh, hear the news?"

"I heard you might have discovered Daniel Stevens' body buried near the old Maple Grove train depot. Is that true?"

"Yes, ma'am, though I wasn't sure who it was. Sheriff Montgomery called this afternoon to say they identified the re...him."

Another woman's voice, this one firm and louder, said, "My grandson knows? Why hasn't he called me?"

Nellie said, "Let me give the phone to my friend, Maryann Montgomery."

"Boy, are you going to be in trouble with my buddy the sheriff. I bet he wanted to tell her himself."

After the sounds of the phone shifting from person to person, Maryann asked, "Do you know who I am, young lady?"

"Young lady? Does she know you aren't so young?"

"I believe you are Daniel Stevens' younger sister. Please accept my condolences."

"Thank you." For a couple of seconds the voice wavered. "I want you to come see me tomorrow, see us."

"Is that...I mean, do you feel up to it?"

"Do I sound feeble?"

"No, ma'am." Digger was beginning to feel like an errant schoolgirl. "Is there something I can tell you now? I mean, I don't know much at all."

"I want you to look me in the eye when you talk to me. Us. Nellie and I are available anytime between nine AM and noon. Can you come then?"

"I..."

"Very well. We'll see you tomorrow." The call ended with a click.

Digger placed the receiver on the wall phone base and leaned her head against the kitchen door jamb.

"What's the matter? Don't you want to talk to her?"

"Sheriff Montgomery specifically said not to get in his way. My guess is that he would consider talking to his grandmother and a former quarry employee just that."

TUESDAY MORNING WAS AT least fifteen degrees cooler, so Digger sat in the driveway for a minute to let her Jeep warm up. Bitsy sat on the back seat, next to Uncle Benjamin.

Digger glanced in the rearview mirror. Bitsy kept looking to his right, and a couple of times he pawed the air. Could he see her uncle? "Why do you always sit in the back seat?"

"If you crash, I'll have a better chance to get out of the car."

"I've never had a single car accident. Besides, you can float out."

She put the Jeep in gear and made her way down the long drive. Before she reached the road, her cell phone rang and she stopped the car. She took it from the side pocket of her purse. "It's Marty."

"Digger, I meant to call last night, but I wanted to check out as much as I could before I wrote the article on the webpage."

Digger had read it, but found it unrevealing. "Did you learn more than what I read this morning?"

"Some. There was a small notice in the paper a few months after Daniel died. It said Isabella Stevens sold her interest in the quarry to Harlan Jones, Leon's father. Didn't make much."

"That's it?"

"I don't exactly sit on my laurels."

"He's a go-getter. You should be nicer to him."

Digger flushed. "I know you don't. You'll never guess where I'm heading."

"Try me."

"Maryann Montgomery called last night. I'm on my way to Oakland to see her and a woman who worked at the quarry when Daniel Stevens was alive."

"No kidding! What does she want?"

"Did I mention I'm on my way there?"

He laughed. "Call me when you get back and we can compare notes."

He hung up before Digger could tell him she didn't plan to take notes. She wanted to meet the women and get to work and her normal routine.

"Maybe you could put your heads together and figure out who offed him."

"Offed him? How well did you know Maryann Stevens?"

"Just in passing, in the store and such. Knew her husband Samuel better. But they moved away, and when they came back to this area they settled in Oakland. Not sure I saw her after, oh, maybe 1970 or so."

"She can't think I know anything. And she can get any information she wants from the sheriff."

"You going to tell her about Brian and his father?"

"She sounds pretty sharp. I bet she knows who they are."

"That's not an answer."

MARYANN MONTGOMERY AND NELLIE PORTER lived in the assisted living component of the sprawling senior complex in Oakland. The woman at the front desk smiled when Digger identified herself. "I'm supposed to take you to Mrs. Montgomery's unit, and then bring tea."

Digger followed her down a carpeted hallway, noting that everything from the paintings along the wall to the doorknockers on the individual units looked expensive.

"Not a bit of character to the place. Everything looks the same."

The woman rapped lightly on unit 124. "Mrs. Montgomery? It's Jenny, with your guest." She opened the door and ushered Digger in without waiting for a response.

"Goes to show you should never judge a person by their voice."

Without getting up, the two women introduced themselves and indicated that Digger should sit on a loveseat across from their matching Queen Ann chairs. Maryann said, "Thank you for coming, Ms. Browning."

While the women had sounded elderly and, in Nellie Porter's case, almost feeble, in person they appeared formidable. Both wore dresses with coordinating gold jewelry. Nellie was rail-thin and her hair was a brilliant white, while Maryanne dyed hers a honey gold.

"Kind of like queens overseeing their courts."

Digger sat across from them on a pale blue loveseat. "It's nice to meet you, though I'm sorry for the circumstances."

Maryann sat up straighter. "I always knew we would learn my brother did not abandon his family. Have you heard anyone say who killed him?"

"Uh, no, but I'm not sure I'd know more than would be in the local media."

"The Oakland paper had a brief article and, of course, the *Maple Grove News* won't be published until Friday," Maryann said. "Their web page said that their reporter was with you. Did you expect to find something under that sundial?"

Somehow, Digger hadn't expected a ninety-year-old woman to use the Internet. "No, Marty Hofstedder thought it would be a local interest story, I suppose, and I wanted to take a couple pictures to use for the historical society. I don't think anyone, anywhere, had a clue that your brother had been…placed there."

Nellie Porter spoke. "Miss Browning, I always believed Daniel met an untimely end. No one wanted to listen to me, but he was in the quarry office the night he vanished."

"The plot thickens."

"What makes you say that? I mean, did he leave you a note or something?"

Nellie shook her head. "Every night I turned the thermostat down two degrees. When I came in Monday morning, it was set for the daytime. I know I left it lower, and Mr. Jones and his wife were away. No one else would have used the office."

Maryann's voice was brittle. "No one would listen to a young woman. They said there would have been tire tracks in the snow."

"But not," Nellie interrupted, "if he was there before it got deep. It would have snowed over them."

"And he never made it to his Knights of Columbus meeting." Maryann said.

The door to the room opened, and Digger assumed it would be Jenny bringing tea. "Speaking of tire tracks, do you have any idea what happened to his car?"

Uh oh.

Sheriff Montgomery's voice spoke over the end of her question. "Digger Browning. I told you to stay out of this."

Maryann turned a steely gaze on her grandson. "Roger, I wouldn't have had to invite her to see us if you'd stopped by last night, as I asked."

Digger's back was to him, and she slowly turned her head. "Good morning, Sheriff. I didn't think I should refuse the invitation."

Nellie Porter came close to giggling. "Maryann's reputation precedes her."

"Sit down, Roger."

Digger almost smiled as the burly lawman took a seat next to her. He seemed more like a kid about to be scolded than a guy who carried a gun and wore a badge.

Nellie spoke before Maryann could. "Now, Roger, when you became sheriff, we both talked to you about Daniel. You said you didn't have anything to go on then."

He nodded, "And I do now." He looked directly at Maryann. "Grandmother, we may never know how your brother ended up in that horrible place, but at least this proves you were right. He did not leave of his own accord."

"At least is not good enough. I want to know who killed him."

"And if there is any forensic evidence, I will use it. But," he spread his hands, "Daniel would be more than 100, his wife is dead and so are any friends."

"I'm asking you to find his most cruel enemy," Maryann said.

"I'd say that sounds more like an order."

CHAPTER ELEVEN

DIGGER LEFT THE TWO women a few minutes after Sheriff Montgomery did. She found herself caring what happened to Daniel Stevens, but she didn't want to get involved in family issues.

The brief article on the *Maple Grove News* website had a quote from Matthew Stevens asking for privacy, but did not mention Brian or the connection to the Montgomery family. Maryann surely knew who they were, but because she hadn't asked about them, Digger figured she might not realize Brian had been looking for his grandfather.

The air had cooled in the short time she'd been in the building, and she drew gloves from the pocket of her down jacket as she left.

"You better get your best grovel face on."

"What does that mean?"

To her right, Sheriff Montgomery said, "Who are you talking to?"

"Oh! Just asking myself a question. I should probably do it silently."

"Digger, you're not normally a nosy person, and I can't tell you what to do or not do. But it's not a good idea to encourage my grandmother in delving into this more."

She faced him. "I have no intention of doing that. I told you, she called me. I was being polite."

He turned toward the parking lot and Digger fell into step beside him. "I would love to find Daniel's killer. Never met him, but heard a hundred stories from my grandmother. But unless someone confesses, we may never know."

"Are you not going to look?"

"Of course I am! We are. But after all this time, there won't be much to go on."

THE UNSCHEDULED MURDER TRIP

"What about the rug? Maybe, I don't know, it's unique and someone will remember it if you publish a photo of it."

Montgomery stopped at his SUV and faced her. "I know how to do my job. I'm sorry you had to find him, but there's no reason for you to be any more involved."

"I hear you." Without saying goodbye, Digger turned and walked to her Jeep.

"Those law enforcement types always park in the fire lanes."

She said nothing.

"Are you going to do anything else?"

"I'm going to work." She opened the door and slid into the driver's seat.

"If I were you, I'd look for stuff beyond Daniel Stevens. Had to be that client of yours put down the gravel."

"Very likely. And Leon Jones and his daughter would definitely keep bringing us business if I walked into Mountain Granite Quarry and asked if that rug looked familiar."

"What's her name?"

"Marilyn Jones. I think her married name is Davis, but she goes by Jones for business purposes."

"You friends with her?"

"We're close in age, but she was homecoming queen in her year, and pledged a sorority at Frostburg. I was president of the Maryland History Club. Different interests."

"Invite her to lunch. Go to the pasta place on Main Street. I loved that place."

"Uncle Benjamin, I have work to do. And I barely know her."

"I remember one time when they were putting in gravel at the depot the ground was terribly muddy. Their dump truck sunk in almost to the top of its hubcaps. Great picture in the paper."

"I saw Leon at the depot the other day. He mentioned something about a picture in the paper."

"So, find out when it was."

"You mean if they were putting in gravel and the ground was that soft, they could have buried his body then?"

"Maybe. I'm not doing all the thinking for you. Go to the historical society."

64

DIGGER CALLED HOLLY WHEN she got into Maple Grove. "If the paper lets us do a short piece on the depot's history, it could get us some good publicity."

Holly almost snorted. "You have a one-track mind."

"I have one thing to look up at the historical society."

"Okay, but you need to stick around all afternoon. I've got appointments at the jewelry store and laundromat."

"The laundromat?"

"They think they can get more business if young people see some sort of social element to being there. I said, 'You mean suds and buds?' and the guy almost drooled into the phone. Wanted me over there today to talk about ideas."

"You're brilliant."

"I know. My grandmother's the volunteer at the historical society this morning. Be on your best behavior."

"I'll do my best." Digger hung up.

"I'll have to, too. Audrey Washington doesn't like me."

"Uncle Benjamin, she can't see you."

"That woman's a witch. She probably can."

"What did you do to make her mad?"

"Big assumption in that question."

"I know you."

"Hmph. Those two new buildings on the square have bigger utility bills than the depot did. They were talking about raising dues, and she said we were turning the society into a club only well-off folks could join."

"Ouch."

"I was about to bring up that we could give scholarships, but that fall down the stairs put an end to that idea."

"Changed a lot of things."

DIGGER PARKED ON THE street across from city hall. The Maple Grove Historical Society had moved to the small town square almost a year ago, but whenever she was headed there she still pictured it in the old train depot.

THE UNSCHEDULED MURDER TRIP

Audrey was indeed at the society's reception desk. Rather than a greeting, she said, "Digger, reach into the front display window and fool with that coal miner's hat. It's crooked."

"Yes ma'am."

The large front window held local memorabilia and other artifacts. The coal miner's hat sat between a model of the first log cabin in Garrett County and a grouping of arrowheads. Because the window had a four-foot tall piece of wood as backing, only a giant could have reached into it easily.

Digger removed the step stool that resided in a small closet near the front door. She balanced on the top step and reached in. The coal miner's hat seemed straight to her, but what did she know? She nudged it a bit and began to climb down.

"One moment, Digger. Let me go outside and see how it looks."

"It's terribly cold. Wear your coat."

"Witches don't need coats."

"I've got my shawl and I'll only be a minute."

Digger hissed. "You can't distract me. I'll fall into the display."

"Too bad your buddy Marty's not around to take pictures."

"If I could touch you, I'd shove you in."

From outside, Audrey said, "What's that Digger?"

"Talking to myself about whether we should redo the display after the holidays."

"Heh, heh. I'm going back to the scrapbook section."

Several minutes and many rearrangements later, Audrey seemed satisfied and came back inside. She pulled her shawl tighter and sat behind the desk, posture ramrod straight, as usual. "I read about you and that Marty at the paper finding poor Mr. Stevens."

"Did you know him?"

"Not well. I worked at the Kresge store on Main Street, and he didn't come in too often. That was before Black and White people socialized too much."

"That's a euphemism if I ever heard one. Even the churches were separate."

She decided to delve into what Audrey did know. "I expect Uncle Benjamin would have known his sister better."

"Maryann, yes. Poor thing. She was so very distraught. Absolutely never accepted that he left town willingly."

Uncle Benjamin drifted into Digger's line of sight. *"Technically, he didn't leave town."*

"I went to the depot to take pictures of the sundial being removed. I thought…"

Audrey pursed her lips. "It's scandalous that they did that when no one was paying attention."

"Not to be a smart-mouth, but do you know anyone who wants a few hundred pounds of a concrete, nonworking sundial?"

"Ooh. Now you stepped in it."

She bristled. "That's not the point, Digger. Seems the Chamber should have needed permission, or something."

"Maybe when it's renovated for the visitor center someone can apply to get it on the National Register of Historic Places."

Audrey nodded emphatically. "Superb idea. That would keep those Chamber people in their places."

Abigail is going to love you for the idea.

Digger excused herself by saying she wanted to find any articles about the old depot. She escaped to two rows of shelves in the very back of the space. She could get articles about Daniel's disappearance from Marty. She wanted to know when the depot parking lot was expanded.

If Daniel died in November, that would have been an unlikely time for regrading and adding gravel. If work got underway in the spring, where was the body hidden for a few months, and by whom?

She hated to think of Daniel's partner as his killer, but he could have placed the body under the sundial. But when was that put in? Someone would have had to move it to place a roll of heavy carpet, complete with a body, under it.

As she sought the *Maple Grove News'* index for spring 1964, Uncle Benjamin suddenly came between her and the shelf.

"Oh my God!"

A shadow appeared and Uncle Benjamin disappeared.

"You okay, Digger?" Marty asked.

She turned and forced a smile and lowered her voice. "Don't tell Audrey, but I thought I saw a mouse scurry across the top of the row of books in front of me."

Marty's eyes traveled to the shelf she had been studying. "If you want articles from the paper, I can get them you know." He inclined his head as if starting a bow.

"Right." She faced him. "I had a thought about when the body could have been put there."

He grinned broadly and his glasses fell down his nose. He pushed them back up. "Just had those tightened last week. Great minds think alike."

"You should at least give him a peck on the cheek."

Digger felt herself start to flush and she turned to the shelf. She pulled out the index that covered 1964-66. "I figure it had to be spring 1964, and I told you Leon Jones mentioned an article about mud."

"I found it on microfilm. Not good enough to use for a copy."

"Look in the damn scrapbooks!"

Digger frowned as if thinking. "I've never paid much attention to all the scrapbooks here. Most are contributed by families." She pointed toward a set of tall shelves along a back wall. Each shelf held over-sized periodicals, scrapbooks, or very old histories.

"Worth a shot. The picture had a detailed caption, but no article. It showed Mountain Granite Quarry's truck getting stuck and said they were going to finish the project in ten days or so, when the ground dried some."

They walked the twenty feet to the taller shelves. "I wouldn't know where to begin," Marty said.

"With the society's master index, Dummy. I mean you're a dummy, not him. You know it's on the computer."

"I just remembered there's a master index on the public computer. We can look under depot, railroad, and mud."

"Or the quarry. Lead the way."

Ten minutes later, they didn't have specific reference to the article, but had realized that until 1979, the scrapbooks were arranged chronologically. After that, they were by one of several subjects. Digger pulled the one for 1964 and they sat side-by-side at a pine table near the shelves. It's glass top covered a lot of pock marks and a few gouges.

Digger opened the scrapbook and Marty leaned toward it. She suddenly felt warm and took off the light wool sweater she wore.

The pages had been placed in plastic sleeves, but years of use without them had left frayed edges. They paged through assorted photos people had submitted from a huge snowstorm in early January and a faded program from a Sadie Hawkins' dance at the Knights of Columbus Hall.

And then Digger turned a page and saw a news clipping of the article Leon Jones had described. His father stood in mud almost up to his calves, arms raised in exasperation.

Marty pointed to the corner of the clipping. "That's the sundial. At the edge of the photo." He took out his phone. "Be on the lookout for Audrey. You aren't supposed to take pictures in here."

"Guy has a good brain. Go up front and ask her a question."

"Be right back," Digger told Marty.

As she neared the small reception area in the front of the society, she could hear Audrey on the phone. "Yes, Sheriff. I expect the microfilm and scrapbooks would have several items."

She almost ran back to where Marty sat. As he stuck his phone in his pocket, she said, "Sheriff's on the way over here. We have to put that away and head out!"

"Why, we could…"

"I'll tell you at the Coffee Engine. "Put it back and follow me."

They walked to the front, and Digger paused at the reception desk. "Call me if you want that coal miner's hat moved again."

Audrey shook a finger at her. "You're making fun of me. You tell my granddaughter to call me."

"Yes ma'am."

Marty came up behind her. "Thanks, Mrs. Washington I need to spend more time in here. If that's okay."

"Membership's twenty dollars a year." She smiled. "If you're going to be here a lot."

"I'll have Holly call you." Digger walked out and turned toward the coffee shop. She looked behind her. "High tail it, Marty."

His bemused expression showed he didn't get the subterfuge, but he fell into step beside her. "You're buying."

CHAPTER TWELVE

THE AROMA OF WARM vanilla and caramel reached Digger as she opened the door to the Coffee Engine. Marty made a show of sitting at a booth while Digger ordered for them at the counter.

"I used to make fun of this place because the coffee smelled like candy. Sure wish I could smell it now."

"So what did Daniel Stevens' sister want?"

Digger placed their mugs on the table and slid in across from Marty and down a few feet. "Unfortunately, the sheriff came in just as I asked about the car."

"You're starting in the middle. Tell me what Maryann Montgomery and her friend had to say."

Digger added the cream to her coffee and relayed the earlier discussion, highlighting Nellie's comment about the thermostat at the quarry office. "He couldn't have come in at a more inconvenient time."

"Because he heard your question?"

"Because I didn't get to hear Maryann Montgomery's answer."

Marty grinned. "You'd be a good reporter."

"It was so long ago, even if the car made it to a scrap yard, it's not like there would be records."

"In some states, they have to record the Vehicle Identification Numbers now, in case the police are looking for a car." Marty blew on his coffee. "Too bad we can't talk to Matthew Stevens."

"I thought you said you were going to sit outside their house and call Brian after the sheriff or whoever left."

"That was the plan, but Deputy Sovern – you know him – drove by and pointed a finger at me. I can take a hint. As I drove away, I saw Montgomery heading toward the Stevens' place."

Digger shook her head. "I'm not sure why I'm even thinking about any of this. Besides the sheriff telling us to butt out, I have plenty of work of my own. And I expect Brian will want some more of my time."

"Because you pulled up a skeleton's finger yesterday? Probably some kind of bonding thing."

Digger screwed up her nose. For fifteen minutes she'd forgotten about touching the remains.

"Any ghost would be offended by that remark."

"Jeez, I'm sorry. Of course, it's not funny."

"Just had a sudden chill." She glanced at the clock on the wall. Instead of numbers, coffee mugs marked the hours. "I need to get back to the office. Holly has appointments this afternoon, so I need to do in-house work."

"I'm going to sit here for a few more minutes. If I find out more, I'll stop by."

Digger decided she'd look forward to seeing him.

DIGGER ARRIVED AT THE office to a scene that would optimistically be called awkward. Marilyn Jones Davis sat in the chair next to Holly's desk. On the surface, it might seem a friendly conversation. Holly's straight spine said otherwise.

Marilyn stood as Digger walked toward them. "I certainly expected you to be in your office today."

Digger forced her face to become impassive. "Expectations and reality don't always coincide. What can I do for you, Marilyn?" She gestured to the customer chair next to her own desk. As Marilyn passed in front of her, her long wool coat brushed Digger's knee. Digger mouthed "sorry" to Holly. Her lack of reaction said she was ticked off.

Marilyn sat, with what could be called a flounce. "Since Mountain Granite Quarry is your biggest customer, our expectations are that we can reach you anytime."

Saying nothing, Digger pulled out her phone and looked at the screen that showed new actions. "I'm sorry, Marilyn, I don't have a text or email that showed you were coming."

She pointed a finger at Digger. "I shouldn't need to let you know."

THE UNSCHEDULED MURDER TRIP

Usually she dealt with Leon Jones, so she'd not seen this side of Marilyn. She probably should have been able to predict it. "Anytime you want to meet here rather than your office, just let me know. Holly and I appreciate your work, but we sometimes need to be with other clients." She forestalled Marilyn's interruption. "Now, what can we do for you?"

She tossed long strands of thick brown hair over one shoulder. "My father said you took some photographs at the depot for our annual report."

"I took photographs, yes. When I ran into him, I asked if he might be interested in one for your annual report. He liked the idea."

"I want all of them."

"I offered one as a courtesy. You could buy the others for a discount. Let's say twenty dollars each."

She stood, her face flushed. "That's ridiculous. After all we pay you…"

Holly raised her voice slightly. "And we appreciate the contract for the brochures and the redesign of the quarry's letterhead. I don't believe they include unfettered access to our work."

"Unfettered. Go Holly!"

Marilyn stood totally still, then transferred her gaze to Holly, who met it and did not look away. "I take your point."

Digger gestured again to the chair next to her desk. "Have a seat. I transferred the files to our computer, but haven't gone over them except to take out a couple that weren't in perfect focus."

"Thank you." Marilyn sat, the flush leaving her complexion, with two red spots remaining on her cheeks.

Digger hoped the woman felt embarrassed. She faced her screen and with a few clicks of the mouse brought up the list of photos she'd placed in a "Depot 2020" file. She hadn't even named them yet. She changed the view so the photos showed. "A lot will look identical to you. I take several from the same position, to be sure I get one I consider as close to perfect as possible."

She tilted the screen so Marilyn could see it better, and slid the mouse to her. "You can click through at your own pace." Digger sat back in her chair. Though she sat several feet from the display, she could see the photos as Marilyn passed through them.

Marilyn's back was to Holly. Digger turned her head slightly and their eyes met. Holly looked at Marilyn for a second, shook her head, and went back to her project.

Marilyn stopped at one photo for several seconds. The first one with the sundial. She scrolled more slowly through the several after it.

"Didn't think she really wanted to look for pictures for an annual report. What would the caption be? 'Here's where the dead guy was, so we covered the spot with gravel?'"

Digger coughed lightly into her hand. When Marilyn paused again over the photo of the empty hole, Digger said, "I was sorry to find your grandfather's partner near where the sundial sat."

Marilyn nodded, but said nothing.

"I'm not sure exactly when your dad was born. Did Leon have a chance to meet Mr. Stevens?"

She stopped clicking the mouse and turned just her head toward Digger. "No, my father was born in 1965. He heard a lot about him from his father. I'm not sure they would have spoken as much about it, but my father had to take over the business after his father got cancer. Grandfather wanted to pass on everything he knew."

"I know your grandfather died in his sixties. Hadn't thought about how young your father would have been when he had to take charge."

Marilyn's nod was perfunctory as she turned back to the photos. "Only twenty-two. It wasn't what he intended to do with his life, but he really built up the business." Her posture relaxed as she scrolled through the rest of the pictures.

"No doubt you'll continue to do the same."

"You've moved from flattery to ass-kissing."

Marilyn looked briefly at her, and then away. "Thank you."

Digger picked up a notepad from her desk and wrote a couple of cryptic notes. Dates, price. She wanted to know when Isabella Stevens sold her portion of the business to Harlan, what she made from the sale (if that could be discerned), and how much the business was worth when Harlan died. She figured the latter might be in probate records at the county courthouse. Then she wrote three words, one under the other. Weeks, Topics, Funds.

"I know what those initials really mean. Naughty, naughty."

Digger dropped her pencil and stooped to pick it up. The action hid her smile. She couldn't get anything past Uncle Benjamin.

Marilyn had finished her review. "I'll let you pick out the specific ones. I'd like one that shows much of the area. You know, the depot, the lot around it. One that's closer and focuses on the building, one fairly close to the sundial, and one that largely shows the hole."

The last request seemed pretty gross, but Digger simply continued to make notes as she talked. "I'll have them printed. I can email your secretary the digital files."

"Send them to me. And the bill should go directly to me, please." She hadn't taken off her outerwear, so when she stood, her long coat flew behind her like a witch's cloak as she walked out the door.

Neither Holly or Digger said anything until they heard her feet reach the first floor. Holly spoke first. "I'm beginning to think the address on our cards should be a post office box."

"Not a bad idea."

"It's a rotten idea. People need to be able to find you."

Digger couldn't tell him she thought Holly was just spouting off. "Holly, I'm sorry you had to deal with her."

"I don't mind, Digger, but it can't be that I'm the inside person and you're the outside person who doesn't have a set schedule. What took you so long at the historical society?"

Digger knew she deserved that. "Marty came in and we compared notes…"

"On what? You aren't a detective."

"Remember, we talked about proposing an article to the *News* that focused on the history of the depot." Digger hoped she could mention it to Marty before Holly spoke to him again.

AN HOUR LATER, DIGGER finished reviewing Holly's draft copy for the laundromat. A washing machine's raised lid had the phrase, "If the buds bring the duds." The front door of the dryer said, "We've got the suds."

"I like it. Do you think a lot of younger people will know what 'duds' are?"

"Won't hurt to expand their vocabulary."

The prior frostiness had left Holly's voice. That was one of the things Digger liked about working with her. They could honestly tell each other what they thought, but nothing was personal.

"Some of the clothes in the attic trunks could use a washing machine. Kind of dusty."

Digger ignored him. "If they like the idea, we could do a few different print ads, maybe a couple of them could be inserted on the local cable channel."

"Right," Holly said. "Too bad we don't get paid by how many times an ad appears."

The landline rang and Digger answered it. "You Think, We Design."

"Digger, this is Leon Jones." Digger mouthed his name to Holly. "Marilyn mentioned that she stopped by."

Uncle Benjamin hovered near the phone. *"I bet she told him what she thought of you."*

"She did. I'm going to pick out a few photos for her."

Leon took a breath. "She's a very good businesswoman, but she hasn't done a lot of customer service-type work."

"That's a euphemism for saying she isn't a people person."

"Don't worry about it. We are going to sell her a few prints, but my offer to give you one for the annual report still holds."

After a pause, Leon said, "I'm so sorry you had to find Daniel Stevens. To think, we were both out there a few days ago."

"Gotta wonder what he was really looking for."

"I know. I've seen the picture of him and your father on the wall in the quarry's reception area."

"My father often spoke of him. He joined the search that first few days. Most people don't know it, but he paid a firm to look for him a couple of times. A few anonymous callers said Stevens was in Pittsburgh or Chicago."

Digger hesitated. "And he obviously wasn't."

"Clearly. He never knew if they were honest tips or not, but when he discussed them, I never thought they were. Who would leave the information anonymously if they were trying to help?"

Holly gave Digger a questioning look, and she pointed to the receiver and shrugged. "I see your point. I guess he told Daniel's wife about the results."

"I'm not sure. There was some…strain when he purchased Daniel's half of the business from her. Well, you can imagine it was difficult. Daniel's sister didn't make it any easier. She wanted Isabella to stay involved so Daniel had the business to come back to."

"Wow. Talk about unbridled optimism."

He sighed. "That's one way of putting it. I wish he'd been found when Isabella was alive. Whatever happened to him, he didn't abandon his wife and children."

CHAPTER THIRTEEN

DIGGER SPENT THE NEXT two days focused on work and trying to keep Uncle Benjamin from accompanying her everywhere.

"Can't you at least stop by the historical society? Bring home something I haven't read."

"You know the society doesn't permit us to check out anything. And you helped write the book they sell. In fact, you have a copy of it here."

"I know what's in the book. You could stick something else in your pocket. You'd bring it back."

"I'll tell you what. I'll print out a lot of articles from the Internet. People publish family histories, historians write a lot about Maryland from roughly the Civil War forward. Especially about the railroads. You could learn something."

"Humph. I'll make corrections and you can email the authors."

As she went to bed Thursday evening, Digger decided she'd come up with an Internet reading list for her uncle and periodically print new items. She felt bad that he was bored being stuck in the house or the building where she worked, but she had to make a living.

THE FRIDAY *MAPLE GROVE NEWS* had Daniel Stevens' obituary and an article that contained interviews with Sheriff Montgomery, Maryann Stevens Montgomery, and Leon Jones. Some of the material had been on the paper's website during the week, but the print edition pulled all of it together.

Uncle Benjamin sat cross-legged on the kitchen table and read the story as Digger did.

THE UNSCHEDULED MURDER TRIP

After giving the basics of Daniel's disappearance and the discovery of his remains – Digger couldn't think of it as a body – the article summarized what little Sheriff Montgomery said.

"We believe the body had to be placed under the sundial when the parking lot was expanded. However, because of weather conditions at the time, work was paused for more than a week. Some people speculated that the firm that regraded the area and added gravel would have had the opportunity to bury the body."

"Gee, that's a wild idea."

"Shush, I'm reading."

"And while that is true, the muddy site was open and no work went on for more than a week. It is also possible that Mr. Stevens' killer saw this as a chance to dispose of the body in a way to ensure it would not be found for decades, if ever."

"I bet Mountain Granite Quarry contributes to his campaign."

Digger looked at Uncle Benjamin. "It's on the edge of town, and no one goes out there at night."

"Except to drink beer. Too bad anyone who could have seen anything is probably six feet under themselves."

"Fifty-six years," Digger murmured. "Be in their seventies at least. And it was so muddy, probably no one went out there for fun that week."

Marty had asked the sheriff questions about forensic evidence. He dodged them well, deferring to the medical examiner and then noting that Dr. Cluster would work with the Maryland State Crime Lab. "As you might expect, there will be little to go on at this point. While Dr. Cluster and state technicians will do their best, it's not a television show. Don't expect a cigarette butt to have survived and provide a killer's DNA."

"Kind of cheeky of him, don't you think?"

"I bet he's tired of the questions."

The sheriff then offered his sympathies to Matthew Stevens and family. Matthew had declined to comment and asked for privacy.

Not so Maryann Stevens Montgomery. "I have always known my brother would not willingly leave his family, farm, and business. In 1963, I did not believe that every effort was made to find him. Perhaps the killer was simply more cunning than the sheriff of the time."

"Yikes," Digger said.

Maryann continued, "But I believe my grandson, Sheriff Roger Montgomery, will do his utmost to unearth my brother's murderer. I plan to give him full assistance."

"Unearth? He's already been unearthed."

"You're terrible."

"Just making a point."

Digger scanned the rest of the article. "The killer probably isn't alive. If he is, he wouldn't be happy to know Mrs. Montgomery is coming for him."

She turned to Daniel Stevens' obituary, on page six. The three-paragraph summary of his life described his roots in the county, his love of family, and World War II service, specifically noting his role in D-Day. The survivors were Matthew's family, that of his sister in Colorado, and Daniel's sister, Maryann. Charitable donations were asked for the Wounded Warrior Project.

Uncle Benjamin stopped Digger as she began to turn the page. *"I think I saw Stevens' name in a letter to the editor on page seven."*

Digger took a look. "That's Maryann Montgomery's friend, Nellie. She sat with Maryann when I met her."

Nellie Porter's letter would fall into the category of 'blistering.' She described her efforts to get "the incompetent sheriff of that time" to focus on Daniel's presence at the quarry the weekend of his disappearance.

"No one wanted to find out where Daniel Stevens went that Sunday night. He didn't go to the Knights of Columbus, and the bartender said Daniel looked kind of angry. Someone turned up the thermostat at the quarry office. I think they would have paid more attention if a man told them."

"That'll make her popular with the guys at the sheriff's department."

"She's probably right about the last part, for back then. But I wonder if it would have made much difference?"

Uncle Benjamin shrugged. *"If they didn't consider it a place he might have gone that night, they wouldn't have looked for blood or something."*

"Or realized that a red rug went missing." She looked at the article again. It didn't mention the rug he had been wrapped in. She supposed they were holding that information back on purpose.

Uncle Benjamin left the table and had gravitated to the large china cabinet in the dining room. Franklin had placed the triangular case containing an American flag, a gift from the U.S. military when they provided the military veteran plaque to sit in front of Uncle Benjamin and Aunt Clara's headstone.

"Wounded Warrior Project deals a lot with mental health issues."

"And physical disabilities, but if he was involved in D-Day, he could have seen a lot of horror."

"Watching anyone die in war is a horror."

Digger said nothing, expecting him to continue, but he didn't. "I'm going to the office. Are you coming?"

Uncle Benjamin continued to stare at the flag. *"Is my son coming up?"*

"No, he was here last week, you know. He usually sends an email on Wednesday or Thursday if he's coming to work on the attic."

"I think I'll stay home anyway. You know how people say they want to dive into a book?"

"I do."

"I can actually do that. Lots of local history books I never read cover-to-cover."

DIGGER ARRIVED AT THEIR second-floor office before Holly and made a pot of coffee. The office voice-mail had a message from Abigail saying the Chamber had postponed the ribbon-cutting at the depot until next week.

"No surprise."

The next phone message was from Maryann Stevens Montgomery, who wanted Digger to visit her late Friday afternoon. She did an internal groan. She and Holly had a meeting with the jewelry store to discuss new store signage, and she wanted to work on the piece for the *Maple Grove News*. Holly had bought into the idea that a history of the depot would certainly be read now, and Digger's short bio at the end of it would let the town know about You Think, We Design.

She left both messages in the digital file so Holly could hear them. She didn't want to drive the rest of the way down the mountain and over to Oakland in the late afternoon. However, a daytime visit would interrupt work. And Maryann's brother was being buried the next day. It wasn't as if Digger could suggest they meet next Tuesday. Or she could, but it would be rude.

Holly listened to the messages. "You going?"

"I will today, but I'll have to let her know I can't usually visit anytime but weekends."

"You think she'll call a lot?"

Digger shook her head. "I guess she feels a link because I found him, but that idea will fade. Plus, I hate to say this, but she's really old. She won't call forever."

Holly grinned as she turned on her computer. "Very rude."

THEY HAD FINISHED GOING over drafts for the jewelry store signs when someone began climbing the stairs. "Sounds like Brian," Holly said.

Digger walked to the door and opened it before he could knock. "Come in Brian. How are you?"

"Okay, I guess. My tests went okay."

Digger had forgotten he had said he had university work. "Glad to hear it."

He nodded to Holly. "But I know that's not what you meant." He made for the chair next to Digger's desk. After she sat near him, he added, "It's so ironic. I wanted to find out what happened to my grandfather, and you found him."

She wasn't sure what to say. "One of life's ultimate coincidences, I suppose. I wish it had ended differently for you."

He stared at the floor for a moment and then back at her. "I guess I never really thought about what I wanted to find. It wasn't this."

THE UNSCHEDULED MURDER TRIP

Digger tried to sound sympathetic. "Is your dad happy? Well, not happy, relieved to find out his father didn't abandon your grandmother and her kids?"

He nodded. "And he had a nice conversation with grandfather's sister, Maryann. She sent," he smiled, "a plant, plus a note. He called her."

"That's great."

He smiled broadly. "She has some pictures for him. They're going to get together sometime." His smile faded. "She didn't realize he was sick."

"How's he doing?"

"Considering everything, not too bad. Luckily, this wasn't a week he was supposed to get chemo."

Holly met Digger's eyes for a moment. She looked away.

"Can I do something for you, Brian?"

He started to get up, and Digger gestured he should stay seated. "That didn't mean go away."

"Good. When this is over, the memorial service and stuff, I'm going to explore my dad's side of the family. I guess they were here right after the Revolutionary War, or maybe not much later. No one ever talked about them, so I had no idea."

"We'll go over to the historical society some weekend, and I'll show you some of the materials that talk about life in the county in the early days. It'll mean more if you can picture how they lived."

He stood. "Are you coming to the memorial service on Saturday?"

Digger hadn't planned on it, but she couldn't say no, so she nodded. "Yes. Is your great aunt coming?"

"She says so. My dad wanted it this weekend, because he's having a good week. You never know about next week. And he kind of joked that grandfather's sister was pretty old, so he wanted to have it when she was still around."

"Oh, my," Holly said.

He shrugged. "First sort of joke my dad's told in months."

"That's good, then," Holly said.

"See you tomorrow." He left, seemingly in a lighter mood than when he'd arrived.

When he reached the bottom step, Digger walked to the window and looked to the sidewalk below. She watched Brian get into a small Ford and then turned to regard Holly. "He really got a lot more than he bargained for."

"So did you."

DIGGER LEFT MAPLE GROVE at three-thirty. At least half of her drive would be in daylight. She had tried not to retain the image of the piece of red carpet with Daniel Stevens' bony finger, but that was harder as she drove to see his sister.

When she'd met Maryann Stevens Montgomery last week, the woman had just learned her brother's body had been found and had been somewhat subdued. Based on what Digger read in today's paper, she was now fired up to urge her grandson to solve Daniel's murder.

Twenty-five years ago, that could have frightened or enraged the killer. Now, the person was probably long dead. No one would know who killed her brother, but at least the murderer couldn't focus his ire on her.

His ire. Digger hadn't thought much about it, but she couldn't imagine a woman being able to kill him, roll the body in a carpet, hide the body for months, and then bury it. Could any one person have done that? Simply digging the hole would have been a huge, back-breaking job. Of course, they hadn't exactly dug a six-foot grave.

And where had Daniel's body been before the ground thawed? The temperatures in the mountains were so much lower than 3,000 feet below that he could have been frozen for months, if out in the open. But if he had been, animals would have gotten to him.

"Ugh." Almost every property, even those in town, had outbuildings beyond a garage. But it would seem most likely that he had been hidden on a country property. Or maybe an unheated cellar. But it would have to be a place no one went besides the killer.

Digger pushed the thoughts aside. She would focus on the beautiful scenery she was driving through. Even with most of the leaves off the trees, the mountain landscape, with occasional pastures and isolated farmhouses, felt peaceful.

THE UNSCHEDULED MURDER TRIP

At Deep Creek Lake, she slowed while driving over Glendale Bridge, which crossed the lake at a narrow spot. The two-lane bridge replaced a one-lane version she'd loved to drive over as a child. The view of the river today could have been from the 1800s. The lower water level looked almost forlorn.

She pulled into the parking lot at the Quiet Spring Senior Complex at four-forty-five. She had stopped at the florist in Maple Grove and bought a thin vase with a single carnation. She took it from the cup holder between the front seats and locked the car.

A new sign graced the front door of the assisted living building. In large red letters, it said, "Masks required." Underneath those words it said, "Mask It or Casket."

"Yikes." Numbers of COVID cases had risen in Garrett County, and the Quiet Spring buildings had apparently gotten very serious about the mask requirement. She agreed with it, but knew some of the independent-minded folks in her rural county did not. She smiled grimly. She didn't need to worry about running into any of them in this building.

Digger took a mask from her coat pocket and put it on before she walked through the door. No one was in the hall as she made her way toward Apartment 124, and she realized people might be in the dining room.

However, as she was about to knock, raised voices came from Maryann Montgomery's apartment. The reedy voice of a woman she didn't recognize said, "Your implication was clear. You want that damned grandson of yours to investigate my family!"

A familiar, younger, voice said, "Grandmother…"

"I can speak my mind anytime!" the older woman said.

Maryann's voice came through, equally loud. "You get out of here, Felicia Jones. And never let me see you again!"

CHAPTER FOURTEEN

DIGGER WANTED TO SINK into the floor, à la the wicked witch in the *Wizard of Oz*. Since she couldn't, she stepped aside as the door opened.

The familiar voice had been that of Marilyn Jones Davis. She pushed a regal-looking woman in a deep purple satin loungewear and a necklace that shouted "diamonds are forever." Marilyn's frown was deep, and her flush grew as Digger stepped aside for the two women to pass.

"Afternoon, Marilyn. Just talked to your dad on the phone not long ago."

Her embarrassment seemed to lessen. "Oh, good. Probably see you next week when you drop off the pictures." She turned the woman's wheelchair down the hall.

Felicia Jones looked at Digger through cataract-clouded eyes. To Marilyn, she said, "Who is this woman?"

Marilyn's voice carried back down the hall. "Someone I work with in Maple Grove."

"What's she doing here?"

Digger stepped into Maryann's apartment and shut the door, so she didn't hear the response.

Unlike the in-charge woman of a few nights ago, Maryann Montgomery had lost all composure. Her cheeks were inflamed and she wiped away a tear with the back of one hand. "Thank you for coming, Ms. Browning."

"Sure." She sat the vase on a table near the door. "Can I get you a glass of water from your kitchenette?"

Maryann sat down and smoothed her tweed skirt. "Put a mug of water in the microwave, would you? Two, if you'd like some tea."

Digger smiled. "Two it is." She kept her back to Maryann as she filled the mugs, thinking it would give the woman time to

85

compose herself. A squat, glass canister held teabags, and one next to it had raw sugar packets. She removed two of each.

When the timer dinged, Digger took out the mugs and inserted the teabags. She turned her head toward Maryann. "You want a sugar packet?"

She forced a prim-looking smile. "Half a packet, please."

Digger did as instructed, and carried the two mugs to the far side of the sitting room. Two coasters sat on the end table between the Queen Anne chairs, and she placed one mug on each.

"Thank you. I'm sorry you had to see me lose my temper."

Digger sat. "No worries. That woman sounded like someone who would drive Gandhi to curse."

Maryann's smile broadened. "Do you know who she was?"

"I doubt there are many Felicias who look about ninety-five, but seeing Marilyn with her gave it away. I had assumed that Harlan Jones' wife had died a while ago." She picked up her mug to take a sip.

"The Devil hasn't collected his due yet."

Digger held the mug in her right hand and steadied it with her left. "Haven't heard that expression in a while. I'm sorry she upset you, especially now."

Maryann waved a hand and then reached for her tea. "I rarely deal with her. We eat dinner in two shifts. She's in the early group, and when I saw that, I specifically asked for the late one."

"She must have been a lot younger than her husband."

"Not too much. Harlan was between Daniel and me, born in 1922. She's close to my age, born in 1928. So she's ninety-two."

"A spring chicken." Digger placed her mug back on the coaster.

"More like a cock's butt."

She laughed. "Say what you really think."

Maryann shook her head. "I'm not usually crude. When Isabella and Harlan decided Harlan would buy her out after Daniel was gone, Felicia worked hard to devalue the business."

"How did she do that?"

"She tried to say the land was worth less, for one thing. I personally went to the county and got the correct information on the assessed value of the buildings and land."

"Good for you!"

She sighed. "I wish Isabella had thought so. I tried to help her get a good price, but I really didn't want her to sell. I was so sure Daniel would," her voice cracked, "come back." She took a cotton handkerchief from a pocket and dabbed her eyes.

Digger lowered her voice. "I'm sorry."

"It was a long time ago." She pocketed the handkerchief. "Isabella was a good woman. If she were alive today, she'd be the first to say she was glad I held onto hope."

"That's good." Digger didn't know why Maryann Stevens Montgomery had wanted to see her, and had no idea what to say.

Perhaps sensing her discomfort, Maryann continued. "When we spoke last week, I of course knew you'd found my brother. I didn't realize Matthew's son had talked to you."

"Yes. It was largely to show him how to use Ancestry.com and other records. Did Matthew tell you that Brian wanted to see if your brother had, um, reappeared somewhere else?"

"He did. He also said that you and that reporter…"

"Marty Hofstedder."

"Yes, Mr. Hofstedder, had cautioned him to be careful not to, I believe it was, ruffle family feathers."

Digger smiled. "Something like that. Especially after he found you on the 1930 census." Then she remembered the 1940 census. "I initially thought you must have died young. You weren't on the 1940 census."

"What do you mean?"

"Daniel and your parents were there, but not you. Did you, I don't know, live with other family for a time?"

After several seconds, she nodded to herself. "Girl Scout camp for two weeks in 1940. That's where I learned to be so independent." She smiled to herself. "I remember the year, because they canceled it from 1941 to 1945. A lot of local men joined the service, and wives either went to work or did double-duty at home."

"Dumb of me not to tell Brian to look for you elsewhere. He was so intent on finding family connections."

THE UNSCHEDULED MURDER TRIP

She shook her head. "I wish we had connected earlier. But I guess it was easier for Isabella to have me out of contact. I was a reminder that her life had not turned out at all as she hoped it would."

"Did she enjoy the farm she inherited from Daniel?"

"Very much. And she was a good dairy farmer."

Digger noted Maryann did not mention any consternation about her brother having inherited the farm. "You moved away for a time, didn't you?"

She nodded. "To Ohio. But we missed the mountains. Home is where your heart stays, even if you leave. When we returned, we went to Oakland rather than back to Maple Grove. It was time to make some new memories."

"That's profound." When Maryann had asked her to drive to Oakland, Digger had been glad Uncle Benjamin had not come to work with her. Now she wished he had. He'd like to see this side of Maryann Stevens Montgomery.

Maryann stared at her for a moment. "I know you largely taught Brian how to look for people, but I asked you to come down today to see if you learned anything about my brother that I might not know."

She shook her head slowly. "I can't imagine I did. Ironically, a few days before the, uh, sundial was moved, I ran into Leon Jones at the depot when I was…"

"What? Was he near the spot where Daniel's body was found?"

"No." More gently, Digger added, "And I guess he was born a couple years after Daniel disappeared. His daughter, Marilyn, mentioned that…"

Her tone sharpened. "How is it that you know the Jones family so well?"

"I met Leon Jones a couple of years ago, when I worked for the Western Maryland Ad Agency. The quarry was my account. When I was laid off, my friend and I started our own graphic design business, and he transferred their business to us."

"When you were coming in, it sounded as if you knew his daughter."

"Marilyn. I went to school with her, but hadn't seen her in years until she came by the office to inquire about the photographs I took at the depot."

Maryann's neck almost snapped as she turned to look at Digger more directly. "Of Daniel?"

"Heavens no! I took some for the historical society, because I'll document the depot renovations. You know, to be on display at the visitor center someday."

"So that's why you were there?"

"No, the first batch of photos was the week prior. That's when I ran into Leon. Then Marty and I heard they were going to remove the old sundial, so we thought we'd take some pictures then, too."

"Why was Leon out there?"

"He said they were going to put in more gravel when the Chamber's contractors finished doing some regrading in the next few weeks."

"Nothing else?"

"Only that when Marilyn stopped by, I asked her if her father had met Daniel. She said no, but that her grandfather had talked about him a lot to Leon. It sounded as if Daniel and Harlan were close." That wasn't exactly what Marilyn said, but close enough.

She smiled. "They did get along." More seriously, she added, "I never seriously considered Harlan would hurt Daniel. They had become good friends. And he was out of town."

Digger thought of something. Leon had mentioned the mud and said they had to stop for a time. Maryann didn't seem to have realized Daniel could have been put in the ground at that time. She didn't want to be the one to tell her.

"May I ask you something?"

"Of course."

"Did you know my uncle, Benjamin Browning?"

"Yes. I should have said I was sorry about his death the first time I met you."

"Thanks. Did you see much of him?"

"No, and after we left Maple Grove, I don't remember seeing him again. Sometime in the 1970s." She shook her head slightly. "He had a reputation for being ornery but honest."

Digger grinned. "Fits him to a T." She opened her mouth to mention that he had told her about Maryann's conversation with Thelma Zorn many years ago. "Did you…" She clamped her mouth shut. "Never mind. I should be getting back."

She had been about to tell Maryann about a conversation she'd had with Uncle Benjamin after he died. No way would she have been able to explain that away.

CHAPTER FIFTEEN

SATURDAY DAWNED CLOUDY BUT CRISP. Digger took Bitsy on a trek through the wooded area behind the Ancestral Sanctuary. Bitsy raced ahead of her, circled back, and charged ahead again.

She kept going over events of the last week. A few days ago, she had barely heard of Daniel Stevens and never met his family. Today she found it hard not to want to learn more about them. At least about what happened to Daniel.

While whoever killed him could be long dead themselves, someone knew something. They could have a thought such as Nellie Porter's, who remembered the thermostat had been turned up in the quarry offices. She wished she had a photo of the carpet Daniel had been rolled in. Red carpets weren't the norm in the early 1960s. She hoped the sheriff would publish a picture or drawing of it.

Her cell phone rang. Bitsy barked and she pointed a finger at him. "It's not for you." She answered.

"Digger? Sheriff Montgomery here."

"Any news?"

"No, and frankly, I'm not expecting any. I called..."

"What about that rug? Can you publish a drawing of it? Maybe someone would remember it from their grandparents' house or something."

"Digger, I didn't call to discuss investigative techniques with you."

"What's up, then?"

"Apparently my grandmother called you again."

"Yes. I promise I don't encourage her."

"Wouldn't matter either way, she does what she does." Montgomery paused. "I called because I think you overheard part of her conversation with Felicia Jones and Leon's daughter, Marilyn."

"Only the yelling part at the very end."

"It upset Maryann. Would you mind telling me what you heard? You're under no obligation to do that."

Digger figured anyone within fifty yards heard it, so why not the sheriff? "I heard Mrs. Jones accuse your grandmother of wanting people to think her family had something to do with Daniel Stevens' death. Your grandmother told her to get out."

Sheriff Montgomery said nothing for several seconds. "Since you do some work for the Jones quarry, I'll let you know we have no evidence that implicates any individual in Daniel Stevens' murder."

"Can I ask you a question?"

"Won't promise an answer."

"You know your grandmother's friend, Nellie Porter? She said she thought Mr. Stevens was at the quarry before he died. Do you think she's right?"

"I don't doubt her memory, but minus anything else, a two-degree change in a thermostat is not a lot to go on."

"What did you think of her letter to the editor?"

He grunted. "Didn't make her overly popular around here, but a lot of people shared her opinion of the sheriff we had fifty-odd years ago. He was what you'd call a good ol' boy."

"One more thing. The county has the ten-person rule on funerals again. Will it be enforced for Mr. Stevens' memorial service today?"

"Since I am the county enforcement, I won't put myself in a position to ignore the law."

DIGGER AND HOLLY STOOD outside the Maple Grove Catholic Church to support Brian -- and in Digger's case, Maryann -- when the memorial service ended.

"When we hear 'Amazing Grace' I think it means they're done," Holly said.

From behind them, Marty spoke. "I hope so, my feet are blocks of ice."

Digger turned her head. "Wondered where you were."

"Finishing a story." He inserted himself in the space between the two women.

They sidestepped a few feet, and each said, "Six feet."

"Oh, right. Sorry. I wanted to finish a feature piece on Daniel Stevens' car."

"Why his car?" Digger thought she knew the answer.

"No one ever found it. That's just too odd."

"Told you that was important. Ask him what he thinks happened to it."

Digger ignored Uncle Benjamin.

"What kind of car?" Holly asked.

"A 1961 Ford Fairlane that he bought at the end of 1960."

"Gene from the Chamber has an old one he drives in parades, doesn't he?" Digger asked.

"Yep." Marty extended his hands. "Big fins."

"What color?" Digger asked.

"Blue. Kind of between a royal and a navy blue."

"You going to look for it, Digger?" Holly asked.

"Funny. I just keep thinking it would be even harder to hide than a body."

From the church came the end of one verse. "'Twas grace has brought us safe thus far, and grace will lead us home."

"There you go," Holly said.

Digger turned to Marty. "Your feet should thaw pretty soon."

"Ghosts don't get cold. Not that I'm advocating you change your status."

The church's heavy wood doors were opened by a funeral home employee in an impeccable black suit. Maryann Montgomery exited first, with Matthew Stevens and Sheriff Montgomery on either side of her. Her erect posture and impassive expression implied total control, but Digger doubted she felt that inside.

Brian and his mother followed, and Digger was surprised to see Leon Jones and his wife, Suzi, stride out behind Brian. No one else came out, which surprised Digger. She knew Matthew had a sister, but perhaps she didn't want to risk being on a plane with COVID raging.

Sheriff Montgomery looked in their direction. Matthew raised a hand, and Digger did the same. He touched his aunt on the arm and pointed to the three of them.

Maryann paused and turned to her left. When she saw Digger, she smiled, then resumed walking.

Holly sniffed and blew her nose. "It's nice to see Matthew Stevens with her."

Digger nodded. "It is. Maybe she'll gain some family even though she lost her brother for good."

They turned away from the church. "Coffee Engine?" Marty asked.

Holly shook her head. "I have a pile of laundry and I promised my grandmother I'd drive her over to Frostburg this afternoon." She left them as they passed her car a block from the church.

Without saying much, Digger and Marty continued to the coffee shop.

"I like him. Good head on his shoulders."

Digger wanted to know more about Marty's thoughts about Daniel Stevens' car, but beyond that she was beginning to appreciate his company more than she used to. She reminded herself she didn't know him that well, and life would be awkward if they dated and then split up.

Marty opened the door to the Coffee Engine and Digger preceded him to the counter.

The bright-eyed barista, a young woman no more than twenty, smiled. "Good morning you two. What'll it be?"

"Get hot chocolate. I want to see if I can smell it."

She nodded to the barista. "I'll have a large hot chocolate with marshmallows."

"I've already had too much coffee. Make mine a latte, no sugar."

They sat across and down a few feet from each other and Marty pulled several index cards from the pocket of his jacket. "I know the odds of anybody identifying his killer are low, but I want to find out what we can."

Digger glanced at the counter. Uncle Benjamin hovered above the barista, nose almost touching the mug of hot chocolate. She turned to face Marty. "I'd like to know more, too. Let me tell you about my last visit to Maryann Stevens Montgomery."

Marty did a low whistle when she finished. "I can't believe I never checked to see when Felicia Jones died. Or didn't. Did she look like someone I could interview?"

Digger shrugged. "She seemed to have her faculties, if that's what you mean. Do you think you should check with Leon?"

He grinned. "I'm better at asking forgiveness than permission."

"She might talk to you if you said you want her to have the chance to say her family had nothing to do with Daniel's death."

The barista brought their latte and hot chocolate, but Uncle Benjamin stayed at the counter, moving among canisters of flavored teabags and buckets of coffee beans. Digger figured he was practicing smelling techniques.

Digger warmed her hands on the steam from her mug and they sat in companionable silence for perhaps thirty seconds. Marty broke it. "Matthew Stevens said he prefers not to talk to me. You think you'd have a shot through Brian?"

"To talk about what?"

"What he remembers from when his father went missing."

"He might be willing to meet me, but my guess is that if I broached that topic I'd get thrown out."

"Tell Brian that finding Daniel was difficult, and you'd like to talk to his son for a few minutes. Say you want to hear some happy memories about him."

Digger met his eyes as she took her first sip of hot chocolate. "Thought a lot about this, have you?"

He grinned. "Some. Maybe ask him if he and his dad did anything special that Saturday."

Uncle Benjamin had come closer and heard the last comment. *"Ask this Matthew for a favor. It's always hard to turn people down when they need a favor."*

THE UNSCHEDULED MURDER TRIP

WHEN DIGGER WENT DOWN to the kitchen Sunday morning, Bitsy sat patiently next to his bowl and Ragdoll had joined Uncle Benjamin on the kitchen table. "Morning everyone."

"Morning. Going to be in the upper forties today."

"Thanks for the weather report. I'm making pancakes. You want me to warm up the syrup so you can try to smell it?"

"I'm giving up on my sniffer for a while. How about we visit one of those ghost towns we talked about?"

Digger had been trying to avoid the ghost town topic. "Exactly what is it you want to do?"

"Just look around. I want to try Kitzmiller first."

She mentally viewed a map of Garrett County, which was the shape of a right-angle triangle with the 90-degree angle at the top left. Kitzmiller sat on the Potomac River, across from West Virginia, midway up the eastern boundary of the county.

"Kitzmiller? I think a couple hundred people still live there."

"They do, but it used to be a lot bigger, and they have this coal museum. I figure we could walk around some, but also visit the museum. Maybe the apparitions there want to hang around a place that looks like the old days."

"I guess that's better than one of the deserted towns you have to hike into. But I need to call Brian Stevens first. I want to talk to his father at some point."

After she finished breakfast, Digger tried Brian's cell, but he didn't answer. "Okay, Uncle Benjamin, we can head down there."

Bitsy barked and thumped his tail.

"Yes, you can come, too." She took a soft-sided, small cooler and put water, granola bars, and an apple into it. When Bitsy wasn't looking, she slipped in a couple of dog biscuits. She added some dry food to Ragdoll's bowl and made sure she had water.

The clear weather made for an easy drive, though on back roads the thirty miles took almost an hour. Uncle Benjamin said little, and moved from the front to back seat and then to the front again. *"Be nice to run into someone down there."*

Digger felt amused. "What would you do? Invite them to come home with you?"

He shrugged. *"I don't even know if other ghosts can change locations. Maybe they have to stay in their old areas, too."*

That got her thinking. What would she do if he did want to have ghost visitors? What if one of them was another man and he tried to peek in the shower? "It gets…complicated, doesn't it?"

Uncle Benjamin shrugged. *"I don't know what to expect."*

TWO HOURS LATER, Digger didn't have to be a mind-reader to see that he was disappointed in the excursion. While she spoke politely to a volunteer at the Coal Heritage Museum, Uncle Benjamin wandered around, occasionally floating through a wall to another room.

Finally, he went to the door, so she felt certain he was ready to leave. Digger turned to the eager helper, a man whose grandfather had worked at a nearby lumber mill more than fifty years ago. "Thanks so much for talking to me. I've always meant to come see what you had."

After he extracted a promise that she would return, Digger walked into the chilly weather. She didn't see Uncle Benjamin, but figured he was in her Jeep.

Bitsy saw her coming and began to bark. "Shhh. Dummy." Digger unlocked the Jeep, got in and opened the small cooler. Bitsy can spot a treat at fifty yards, and tried to put his nose in the cooler.

"Okay, here you go." She barely had the biscuit in her hand when he chomped it and swallowed in one bite. She started the engine and pretended to reach into the back seat to retrieve something. "Where are you?"

Because of the time she'd accidentally left him by the depot, she knew not to drive away without him. After a minute she backed out of the parking space and approached the driveway to exit. Still no Uncle Benjamin.

She put the Jeep in park and pretended to answer her phone, ever the good citizen who didn't drive and talk.

Behind her, Uncle Benjamin said, *"Thanks for waiting."*

Digger jumped and dropped her phone between the seat and the driver's door. "You scared the daylights out of me!"

"Sorry."

THE UNSCHEDULED MURDER TRIP

Bitsy climbed into the back seat, sniffing everything.

She glanced in the rearview mirror as she put the car into drive again. Uncle Benjamin wore a glum expression. "Did you have any luck?"

He sighed. *"I thought so, but maybe it was my imagination. I kept thinking someone was just ahead of me, a woman in a long dress. But I could never quite catch up."*

Digger thought for several seconds. "You're new at this. Maybe there's some kind of etiquette you're supposed to follow."

"Never been big on etiquette."

She smiled to herself. "Where did she go?"

"Toward the river, I think. I started to follow, but I didn't want to get left behind again."

"I promise I'll always look for you." When he didn't respond, she said, "Maybe ghosts only talk to people who lived at roughly the same time they did. You said she had a long skirt."

He sighed. *"In that case, I'll be alone for a long time. I could bump off somebody, but the only folks I'd want to exterminate would be people I don't want to hang around with."*

CHAPTER SIXTEEN

DIGGER TRIED BRIAN again when they got home. This time he answered.

"Hi. I saw you on my phone log. Dad and I went down to visit Maryann today." He laughed. "I have a grand aunt I never knew about."

"That's great."

"She had pictures of Daniel when they were little, and one photo of her with both of my grandparents, dad, and her. I took pictures of the photos with my phone."

"Neat. That kind of leads into what I wanted to talk about. Do you think your dad would talk to me? Even for five or ten minutes."

His tone became cautious. "Maybe. Why?"

"I guess this will sound dumb, but the only memory I have of your grandfather is, uh, finding him. I wanted to ask your dad to share a couple happy thoughts."

"Oh."

Digger spoke faster. "To think of him as a person rather than a body. But if it wouldn't be good to ask him, I won't."

Brian was silent for several seconds. "I get what you mean. I'll ask him. No guarantees."

"Thanks. No rush. Pick a time when it's convenient."

When they disconnected, she figured she'd probably never get to talk to Matthew Stevens.

Uncle Benjamin had been prowling a bookshelf in the living room. He drifted over to her. *"What are you up to?"*

"Just what I said."

Ragdoll wound herself around Uncle Benjamin's ankle.

"My gosh, she does see you!"

He leaned over to stroke her, and she walked off. *"I'm real sure of it. But she doesn't like me to touch her."*

Digger thought that odd. A couple of times she touched him on the shoulder or even bumped into him. She felt nothing, and had never asked if he did. "Are you, I don't know, cold or something?"

He shook his head. *"I don't know."* Uncle Benjamin reached over and tugged on her braid. *"Feel that?"*

"Nope."

"Back to my question. What are you up to?"

Digger sat on the couch and Uncle Benjamin settled into an easy chair across from her. It reminded her of sitting there discussing with Sheriff Montgomery how she found her uncle's body. Except she'd been in the easy chair.

"Okay, I'll tell you. But it isn't anything bad. Marty's going to talk to Felicia Jones down in Oakland…"

"That prickly woman's alive? I figured she'd died long ago."

"You knew her?"

"Not well. And rarely saw her after they built that monster house near Bloomington. But the business was here, so she and Harlan came to Maple Grove. Him often."

"Huh. Anyway, we agreed I'd see if Matthew would talk to me. Not to ask police-type questions, just tell me something about Daniel."

"And what is the other half of 'we' going to do?"

Digger flushed. "Marty's going to tell Felicia Jones he'd like to interview her, give her a chance to say that her family had nothing to do with Daniel Stevens' murder."

Uncle Benjamin shook his head slowly. *"You should think about it some more, before you two start asking questions."*

"Because Sheriff Montgomery won't like it, you mean?"

He snorted. *"That's a given. Because even if the killer's dead, he didn't do it all alone. Someone has kept a secret for a long time, and they aren't going to want you two spilling the beans."*

DIGGER AGREED WITH Uncle Benjamin, but she couldn't imagine that someone old enough to have been involved in Daniel Stevens's death would be able to hurt her today. A voice in the back of her brain reminded her that Leon Jones could have been told something, or stumbled across something that incriminated his parents. If so, he would likely want the secret to stay buried.

She shuddered. Buried like Daniel. She looked at the peeler she was using to pare the carrots. She didn't even know how he died. The *Maple Grove News* website said they would have to send his remains to a state forensic lab to do more than Dr. Cluster and his staff could do in Garrett County.

Her cell phone rang and she put the knife on the draining board and dried her hands. "Hello?"

Brian sounded cheerful. "Hi, Digger. My dad said he'd be happy to meet you."

"Great. No rush…"

"He said come on over this evening. How's seven o'clock?"

"Seven's good. I'll see you then."

Uncle Benjamin floated by as she hung up. *"Remember what I said."*

DIGGER SENT MARTY A TEXT letting him know she was meeting with Matthew, but didn't hear back before she left the Ancestral Sanctuary. The air held a hint of snow, but last time she'd glanced at the weather on her phone it indicated only flurries.

She drove into Maple Grove at six forty-five. Several shops already had Thanksgiving decorations in their windows, and the lone women's clothing boutique had a Christmas tree as well as a fall wreath.

Tiny white lights sparkled in the second-floor picture window at You Think, We Design. Hard to believe that six months ago, she and Holly had lost their jobs at the Western Maryland Ad Agency, and now they had their own business.

"Who put up the lights?"

"I bought them and Holly and I put them up together the other day. Must have been one of the days you stayed at home."

"I'd like to be there tonight. Too cold out here."

"I thought you didn't get cold."

"It's the principle of it. Nights like this are for hot cider and a fireplace."

THE UNSCHEDULED MURDER TRIP

"You could have stayed home."

Digger drove through the small business district and turned onto Lake Street. She parked a couple of houses down from the home of Matthew and Sylvia Stevens. The two-story brick home was more than a firefighter might be expected to own, but she figured he had inherited some of the proceeds from his family's dairy farm.

Brian opened the front door of the center-hall colonial and beckoned for Digger to enter. "My parents are sitting by the fireplace. They're looking forward to meeting you."

They stood as Digger entered the room, and she pulled up her mask. They had been sitting on one of two facing loveseats, and on a coffee table in front of them sat several framed photos. Digger couldn't see who they included.

Sylvia smiled broadly and gestured to the loveseat opposite her and Matthew. "It's so good to meet you. Brian has told us how you helped him."

"It's good to meet you. I knew your grandfather somewhat. I'm sorry you lost him," Matthew said.

"Thanks." She smiled. "Sometimes it feels as if he's still wandering around that big house."

"You bet your bones it does."

Sylvia asked several questions about Digger and Holly's business, then turned toward her husband. "Wasn't the space they're in once where the Lions Club met?"

"Plus a couple other service clubs. Kiwanis, I think. And the Shriners, the ones who raise money for the that hospital that serves kids."

Sylvia laughed. "That's right. And they used to compete for best costume in the 4th of July parades."

Uncle Benjamin had been wandering the room, studying books on two sets of shelves. *"Glad they left me their costumes."*

Matthew reached for one of the framed photos. "I'm glad you wanted to see some pictures of my dad and me. He was always so proud of his kids." He handed Digger the picture.

A young man stared at her from a photo taken earlier than the one in the *Maple Grove News*. He held a little girl about two years old, and next to him, holding a fishing pole, was a boy of about seven. Matthew still had the same alert eyes, though very thin brown hair. Digger realized his sparse hair could have been the result of his cancer treatments.

She smiled. "Uncle Benjamin took my sister and me over to Deep Creek Lake a few times. I wasn't big on putting worms on hooks, but other than that it was great."

Matthew took back the photo she extended. "We went there some, but mostly we'd drive down to the Potomac River. There are a lot of spots where the banks aren't steep. Some you can go down a short bank and stand on a strip of packed dirt. In the summer, anyway."

"Ask him if he went to any of the ghost towns."

"I know there used to be a lot more towns down there. Some coal mining towns, I think."

"More than a few, in Garrett County and across the river in West Virginia. The last place we fished was near the Jones' new home in Bloomington. We went down there several times the last year he was alive." Matthew looked down and shook his head.

"I'm sorry, I didn't mean to make you think about something sad."

He looked up again. "Those were fun trips. My mother, her name was Isabella, always made fresh butter to take, and Felicia Jones would bake bread."

"Ah. I, uh, met her briefly at Maryann Montgomery's apartment."

He laughed. "I heard about that. Those two gals are oil and water."

Digger didn't detect a trace of animosity, or even dislike, for the Jones family. It didn't seem Matthew had grown up suspecting his father's partner had anything to do with the so-called disappearance.

She smiled. "What is your best memory?"

"Hmm. Dad was quiet. He read a lot. Mom always entered stuff in the county fair. I think she was the only woman who would enter cows and cakes." He looked at a space above Digger's head and smiled. "Dad made one of the cakes one year. I guess it was the last year. But he wouldn't let mom put his name on it."

Brian laughed. "I never heard that story."

"I'd forgotten it. Probably forgot more than I remember." He sighed. "I wish I hadn't spent so much time being angry at him for leaving us."

Sylvia put a hand on his knee. "You didn't know."

He nodded. "And I missed him a lot."

"It's good of you to talk to me. I have some positive things to think about now."

Mathew grew somber. "I'm so sorry you had to find him."

Digger chose her words carefully. "I am too, but I'm glad you know what happened."

He shrugged. "We'll never really know, but at least I know he didn't wander around as a homeless guy in some big city."

"Jeez, Dad, I never heard you say that."

Sylvia's voice was firm. "The important thing is that he didn't abandon you and your mom and your sister."

Matthew leaned over and kissed her cheek. "My strong wife."

Digger stood. "Again, thank you. This has been a treat."

The three Stevens stood, and Matthew said, "Don't let my aunt give you a lot of guff."

Digger laughed. "I like her."

Matthew smiled back. "I do, too."

Brian walked her to the door. "Can I come by for another research lesson sometime?"

"Sure. Family history bug is catching, isn't it?"

Digger waited until Brian had shut the door and she was crossing the street. "Are you with me?"

"Yep. If you'd have stayed longer, I could have looked around more."

"What were you looking for?"

"Didn't know, but what I found is interesting."

"Like what?"

"Matthew Stevens talks like he doesn't have a care in the world, but on their dining room table he's got some old files. Couple of them deal with the sale of Isabella's half ownership of the quarry."

"Kind of like he's getting rid of old papers?"

"Don't think so. Two things sitting next to each other are asset statements for the business. One looks like a report Daniel might

have had, the other is the quarry's annual report for about two years after he died. Looks as if the company went up a lot in value after Isabella sold her portion."

"I'm surprised Matthew kept all that."

"He didn't. The name Montgomery is on top of the annual report. Looks as if Maryann was keeping track even if Isabella wasn't."

CHAPTER SEVENTEEN

AS SHE DROVE HOME, Digger thought about the implications of what Uncle Benjamin saw. Had Maryann tried to show Matthew his family had gotten stiffed by the Jones family? Or was she simply sharing some files she had?

Digger's cell phone rang.

"Aren't you going to answer?"

"We're almost home, it can wait. Probably Marty."

"You don't want to keep him waiting too long, he might give up."

"Uncle Benjamin!"

He chuckled. *"You like him more, I can tell."*

"Mind your own business."

"You should talk. Are you going to leave this Daniel Stevens' affair alone now?"

"I suppose. Maybe it depends on what Marty finds out from Felicia Jones."

They drove in silence for a minute. Uncle Benjamin floated into the front seat. *"How much do you think that place costs? In Oakland. Where those two women live."*

"I don't know. Several thousand a month, no doubt."

"I could see Maryann having a good bit of money if she and her late husband sold their insurance firm. But where do you suppose Felicia gets forty to fifty thousand per year?"

"What do you mean?"

"Leon might have bought her out, but I can't imagine it would be for hundreds of thousands of dollars. Even if it's a profitable business, it's not like he'd have a lot of cash lying around."

"Huh. They had that big house in Bloomington, right? Maybe they made a lot when they sold it."

"Hard to imagine, but that'd be easy to find out. I told you, it's always about money."

THE HOUSE PHONE RANG as Digger unlocked the front door.

"I'd say I'd get it, but he wouldn't hear me."

"Funny." She grabbed the receiver from the kitchen wall phone. "Digger here."

"Marty on this end."

She smiled. "I've had an interesting day, how about you?"

"Felicia Jones agreed to talk to me. She's what I think you'd call a piece of work."

"She gave that impression Friday night. What did she say?"

"I have pages of notes. I want to put them in some semblance of order. Basically, she said Maryann Stevens Montgomery is a shrew, and she strongly implied that Daniel had been embezzling from the quarry."

"What? Surely that would have come out."

"I don't know. Coffee tomorrow?"

"Let's say around lunchtime. I don't want to leave Holly in the lurch."

"Okay. Did you meet Matthew Stevens?"

"And his wife. They were delightful. I'll fill you in tomorrow." She hung up.

"Can I come?"

"Only if you promise to behave."

DIGGER BEAT MARTY TO the Coffee Engine for lunch on Monday. She generally only bought coffee, so had to study the limited menu for a moment. "I'll have the three-bean soup and half of a turkey sub."

"I hope you plan on spending the afternoon by yourself."

"On second thought, make it tomato soup."

She sat in a booth and glanced around the shop. Gene and Abigail sat at a table across the room. She waved. "Didn't see you guys."

Gene wiped his mouth with a napkin and ambled over, holding his thick parka as if he carried a baby in the crook of his arm. "Afternoon, Digger. I think we're going to reschedule that ribbon cutting for late this week. You be around?"

"I should be. Abigail can let me know. Were you able to start some of the work?"

He shook his head. "I get that Sheriff Montgomery has a job to do, but I don't know why we had to stay away for a week."

Digger shrugged. "I'm surprised there hasn't been more out-of-town media hanging around."

Abigail walked over. "Too cold for them. I heard the Stevens didn't have the funeral home post the time of the memorial service because they didn't want to attract a crowd."

"That makes sense."

Gene swung his coat over his shoulders, barely missing Digger's cup of coffee. "Don't know why they needed the funeral home. Not like they had the body."

Digger winced.

"That guy would say the wrong thing if he was giving a toast at a wedding."

Abigail said, "Gene, we have to work on your ability to be tactful."

"Huh? Oh." He looked around the room. "Nobody else…ah, here's Marty."

"There's a potential groom."

Digger frowned. She was getting tired of Uncle Benjamin's and Holly's jokes about her getting together with Marty.

Marty declined to shake Gene's hand and offered an elbow bump. Gene wasn't able to raise his arm high enough.

"That man has got to do something about his weight or he'll be lying in a funeral home."

Gene started to ask Marty about an article he wrote about restaurants going out of business, but Marty pointed to Digger. "Can't keep my date waiting."

Abigail's eyebrows went up and she made a thumbs up sign behind Gene's back.

Digger couldn't call out that it wasn't a date, though if she was honest with herself, she'd looked forward to this lunch more than any dates she'd had in the last year.

As Gene moved toward the door, Uncle Benjamin – who'd been hiding behind him – came into view. He laughed and drew a heart in the air.

Marty finished his order and brought Digger's with him when he came over. "Figured I'd save Janet a trip."

"Thanks." Digger grinned at his red face. "You've given Abigail something to talk about for a week."

He took off his jacket and slid it across the booth seat as he sat. "Sorry about that. Didn't mean to ruin your reputation."

She laughed. "You're forgiven." She ate a spoonful of soup, aware Marty continued to regard her. "What? Did I dribble?"

"If the movies were open, I'd try my hand at asking you to go again."

Digger could feel herself flush. "When they're open, we can go together to celebrate."

"*About damn time.*" Uncle Benjamin floated to the pots of soup.

Marty grimaced and pulled some three-by-five cards from his breast pocket. "To get past the awkward part, let me tell you what I found."

Digger reached into the pocket of her jeans and pulled out her small notebook. "You're on."

"First, she seemed to assume I thought her husband killed Daniel Stevens. Why assume that?"

"You said you were going to tell her you wanted an interview so she could say her family wasn't involved. Or something like that."

"Yeah, but that was a bad idea. Instead, I said I knew she and her husband had been friends with Daniel and his wife, as well as business partners. I asked if she wanted to share some memories."

"So with that question she declared her innocence?"

"She mentioned just what the newspaper said back then. She and her husband had been shopping in Pittsburgh. They came home late that Saturday instead of staying over until Sunday."

"Because of the assassination."

"Right. But because she and Harlan didn't live in Maple Grove anymore, I assumed they weren't in town. They were."

"What do you mean?"

"They had left their kids with friends in Maple Grove, and planned to pick them up and drive down to Bloomington."

"Oh, but it snowed a lot."

"Exactly. So they stopped at the friends' house to get the kids, and decided they'd stay in the hotel, the one that's been converted to apartments."

"Used to be called the Land Grant Inn," Digger said.

"Yep. But the kids wanted to stay with their friends, so Harlan and Felicia went to the hotel alone, planning to pick up the kids the next morning."

Digger sat up straighter. "So maybe no one paid attention to what they did that night."

"Possibly. Felicia talked about going to bed early, because they were tired after shopping Friday and much of Saturday."

"She and Harlan heard nothing about Daniel's disappearance until Isabella Stevens finally tracked them down about two Sunday morning. Felicia drove out to the Stevens' farm to be with Isabella. Harlan – get this – went up to the office to check to see if Daniel was there."

Digger pushed her empty soup bowl aside. "I keep forgetting they'd already moved to Bloomington. So it was just a coincidence they were even in Maple Grove?"

"If you believe her."

"Why wouldn't I?"

Marty moved his notecards so the barista could put his soup and a cup of coffee in front of him. "Thanks, Janet." When she'd moved away, he added, "What she said makes sense, it's just that she talked so much. As if she had to convince me, not just tell me."

"You said something about her implying Daniel embezzled some money."

"She talked about, and I quote, 'the books being short.' When I asked by how much she waved her hand and said she didn't bother with the numbers, it was something Harlan looked into."

"I guess any proof would have…" Digger's mind went to what Uncle Benjamin had seen on Matthew and Sylvia Stevens' dining room table.

"What?"

"Just something Uncle Benjamin used to say. Whether you were talking about a vacant house burning, a business being robbed, somebody's estate. He'd say 'it's always about the money.'"

"He had a reputation for being stingy."

From next to Digger's ear, Uncle Benjamin said, *"Who the hell said that?"*

She started. "He was thrifty, but then he'd do something like pay for the historical society's new space."

Marty stared at her for a second. "So you think there could be something to the embezzlement idea?"

"Something in reverse seems more likely. If Harlan Jones and Daniel Stevens were partners, why did the Jones have a huge house by the river and Daniel and Isabella lived on his parents' farm?"

"It's one angle, but hard to prove either way. It's not a public company, so their books don't have to be audited by an outside firm."

"They probably had some sort of annual report. At least, they do one now."

"A lot of financial data?"

Digger shook her head. "It mentions if they got big government contracts and gives a dollar figure for profits. That's about it."

Marty picked up one card and studied it. "If one of them was taking money from the till, the profits should have gone up a lot the next couple years."

"Good point. Anything else from Felicia?"

"Not much. She talked about how her husband joined the search of the area. I guess they scoured the area a lot the first few days. It was cold, and they thought if he was stuck in his car somewhere, they needed to find him fast. Your turn."

"Didn't learn too much about the Stevens. I used your idea of asking for a favor and…"

"Wasn't my idea, but that's a good one."

"Right. Brian wasn't sure his dad would want to talk about even happy things about his father, but they invited me right over. In fact, they'd been down to Oakland to visit with Maryann yesterday."

"Interesting how quickly they picked up on the relationship," Marty said.

THE UNSCHEDULED MURDER TRIP

"My guess is that knowing Daniel was murdered brought a lot of healing. Maybe…" Her phone rang. Digger glanced at caller ID. "Maryann, of all people."

"Digger? Please come down here. It's important."

She rolled her eyes at Marty. "I do need to get back to work, but I could come this evening."

"No. It's urgent. Can't you close your office for the afternoon?"

Marty could hear Maryann's excited voice and did a gimme gesture. Digger handed him the phone.

"Mrs. Montgomery? This is Digger's friend Marty. May I come instead?"

Silence.

Marty shrugged and handed the phone back to Digger.

"Maryann, I'll check with my partner and see if I can drive down in a few minutes. That would put me there in about an hour."

"Thank you." She hung up.

Digger dropped the phone in her purse. "I'll have to talk to her about my schedule. I get that this is an upsetting time for her, but I can't run around the county every day."

Marty took a couple bills from his wallet. "I'll leave the tip. You want to ride down together?"

"I'm not sure she'll see you."

"If she doesn't, I'll take some pictures of the courthouse and outside of the jail. I use Oakland pictures a lot."

TWENTY MINUTES LATER, WITH Holly's advice to tell Maryann that Digger's partner needed her in the office, Digger walked down the stairs and out the door of You Think, We Design and got into Marty's waiting Toyota Camry. "Thanks for driving."

"Holly okay with it?"

"Not really, but I promised to talk to Maryann about spur-of-the-moment invitations."

"You gotta admit, this is a lot more interesting than sitting in your office."

After talking for a few minutes about Daniel Stevens and his varied family members and partners, conversation was thin. They moved to banal topics like the weather and whether the NFL would be able to play its season.

"Why don't you ask him his shoe size?"

Digger smiled. Uncle Benjamin disliked chit-chat.

"What's so funny?"

"Just thinking about how easy it is to run out of things to say."

"Rub it in, why don't you?"

She turned toward Marty, still smiling. "I didn't mean it in a bad way. It's just…life."

"And in this case, one guy's death."

They drove into Oakland at almost two o'clock. A sheriff's deputy stopped them at the entrance to Quiet Spring's parking lot. "Sorry folks, the building's closed except to residents."

Digger didn't know this deputy. At probably less than thirty and looking as if he lifted weights, she figured he was a new hire. She leaned closer to Marty so she could talk through the driver's window. "Sheriff Montgomery's grandmother called me about an hour ago. She said it was important."

"Huh. Well, he's here so I can ask him. Pull partway down the block and walk back."

Marty pushed up his window. "What the hell?"

"Can't be something with Maryann, we just talked to her."

"You can kick the bucket in an instant. I should know."

They walked quickly, Uncle Benjamin alternating between walking and floating in front of them. As they drew near the deputy who'd refused their entry, the medical examiner's van went by and was waved into the lot.

"Damn, now I'm worried," Digger said.

"There's so many what they call fragile elderly in there, I bet a couple people die every month. Especially now."

"Yes, but if it's natural causes I think they take them to a funeral home. Maybe the hospital for an autopsy, but I'd bet not often."

"Good point."

They stopped on the opposite side of the street to the deputy who regulated entry. He saw them and waved them over. "Sheriff says you guys are okay. He wants you to go to his grandmother's apartment."

THE UNSCHEDULED MURDER TRIP

They quickened their pace. Marty pushed his glasses up his nose. "Can't be anything bad with Maryann. They wouldn't let us into her apartment."

Usually, a few residents sat in the lobby, but not now. Jim Sovern, a deputy Digger and Marty knew, stood on the far side of the lobby. He pointed down the hall behind him.

"What happened?" Digger asked.

"Friend of Mrs. Montgomery's died suddenly." He shrugged. "She's convinced it's murder. Not sure anyone else is."

"I'm going to look around." Uncle Benjamin headed toward the dining room.

Marty looked to Digger. "Who was that woman you met the first time you came down?"

"Nellie Porter. She's actually the one who called me."

"You knew her?" Sovern asked.

"Guess we know who died," Marty said.

CHAPTER EIGHTEEN

SHERIFF MONTGOMERY SAT NEXT to his grandmother on a blue loveseat festooned with doilies. He looked as much as if he belonged in such a feminine room as a snake slithering around a kindergarten class.

Maryann's bowed head rested on one hand, with her elbow sitting on the other arm, which stretched across her midsection. Sheriff Montgomery spoke softly to her, though Digger couldn't hear what he said.

Marty knocked lightly on the doorjamb and they both looked up. "Come in Digger, Marty."

They each took a seat in one of the Queen Anne chairs Maryann and Nellie had sat in the night Digger met them. "What happened?"

Maryann said, "It's Nellie."

Sheriff Montgomery patted his grandmother's knee and stood. "Digger, how about you sit over here? I need to borrow Mr. Hofstedder for a minute." He pointed to the door to the hallway, and Marty followed him out. He shut the door behind them.

Uncle Benjamin came into Maryann's apartment, through the closed door.

Digger sat next to Maryann, and on impulse, reached over to touch her shoulder. "I'm so sorry. Are you okay?"

Maryann sat up straighter, and Digger withdrew her hand. "No. If I hadn't pushed Felicia Jones about Daniel's death, Nellie would still be here."

"Did you, uh, talk to her together?"

"Separately. Nellie worked for him and had really liked Daniel. Felicia came down here, this is the night you were here, because Nellie accused her of knowing what happened to Daniel."

THE UNSCHEDULED MURDER TRIP

Digger wanted to ask more about that confrontation, but if Sheriff Montgomery came back in and caught her, she'd be toast. "What happened today?"

She half turned to face Digger. "We usually walk down to lunch together. I'm closer to the dining room, so she stops here for me. When she didn't come, I walked down the hall and knocked on her door."

Digger heard a hospital gurney trundle past. She hoped Maryann didn't recognize the sound.

Maryann stood and walked to her window, which looked out on a patch of grass that held a bench, beyond it the parking lot. "I started to go in – no one locks their doors during the day – but something told me not to. I came back here and called down to the resident manager's office."

"And they found her?"

She turned from the window. "Yes. They think she fell and hit her head on the corner of the kitchenette counter." She nodded toward her own.

"And you think that's...unlikely?"

"I do. She was much more agile than I am. And she was so careful. Neither of us wanted to move to the nursing home unit."

Digger nodded. "The first time I was here I made you some tea. Would you like some?"

In an irritable tone, she said, "Why does everyone think tea will help?

"People want to be doing something for someone who's hurting. There's almost always a teabag within reach."

"Well said." She returned to the loveseat and sat. "I'd love a cup of tea."

As Digger finished putting the teabags in mugs of hot water, Sheriff Montgomery and Marty came back in. She raised one mug. "You want some?"

"No thanks," Montgomery said. "Join us, would you, Digger?"

She put the teabags into the sink and carried the two mugs toward Maryann, who pointed to two coasters on a table near the sheriff. He obligingly put them on the coffee table and Digger sat the mugs on them. She sat next to Maryann again.

Sheriff Montgomery spoke as he lowered himself into a chair facing them. "Thanks for coming down." He nodded at Marty, who sat in the chair next to his. "I explained to Marty that you're here as my grandmother's friends, not as a reporter and," he smiled slightly, 'amateur sleuth.'"

Digger smiled in return and Maryann said, "Mr. Hofstedder, I know who you are, of course, but I don't think we've been formally introduced. Thank you for coming."

"Sure. Sorry for the reason."

"Grandmother, I'm sorry to say that you may be right about Nellie's death not being an accident."

"I knew it!"

"The medical examiner said the wound on the back of her head…"

Maryann winced.

"…is such that she would have had to throw herself backward into the corner of the counter. In other words, she hit it with more force than someone would propel themselves."

"Looks like he isn't going to tell you one of her dining table chairs was overturned."

"So she was pushed?" Digger asked.

"Did you talk to Felicia Jones?" Maryann asked.

With seemingly practiced patience, Montgomery said, "Grandmother, she would never have the strength to do that. Besides, she barely walks."

"Then it was her son, or his daughter, what's her name?"

"Marilyn," Digger said. "Is she down here today?"

Sheriff Montgomery hesitated before saying, "Not that I know of, and Nellie was at breakfast."

Marty pushed his glasses further up his nose. "Is there a lot of crime in this building?"

"No," Maryann said.

Sheriff Montgomery smiled slightly. "Grandmother, we will interview everyone in the building who can get around independently. And I've already called the building's security firm. Someone from my office will look at the film from that hallway."

Marty said, "Mrs. Montgomery, if you'd like Digger to stay down here for a while, I can come back to get her later."

Sheriff Montgomery briefly looked between Digger and Marty. "I have a sister who lives in Frostburg. She's on her way down here."

"That's good," Digger murmured. She hadn't wanted to spend the afternoon with Maryann Stevens Montgomery, but she wished she had been able to have a longer conversation alone.

AFTER THEY'D DRIVEN A mile in silence, Digger took her cell phone from her purse. "Not a good signal through here," Marty said.

"I need to call Marilyn Jones. Marilyn Davis." She pulled up her contacts list.

"I'm not one to back off, but that sounds like one of those 'don't interfere' actions the sheriff warned us about."

Digger shrugged. "She's my client. I'm letting her know her grandmother may have had a tough morning."

"As in murdered someone?"

"Not what I planned to say."

When Marilyn didn't answer, she left a message. "Marilyn. Digger here. I was just at your grandmother's building. In case you haven't heard, someone there died this morning. I know Maryann Stevens was upset. I thought if you hadn't heard, you might want to give your grandmother a call." Digger pushed end.

Marty's tone was noncommittal. "Lots of grandmothers."

"It is a senior citizens' complex." Digger stared out the car window at the dusting of snow that still clung to trees. "Did the sheriff tell you anything more?"

"Nope. He mostly wanted to tell me if I repeated anything Maryann said he'd have my ass on a platter."

"And you agreed to that?"

"Sure. She doesn't know anything. I'll talk to other people."

"Exactly what I would do."

THE ANCESTRAL SANCTUARY FELT bereft Monday evening. Evenings were always tough for Digger these days.

Much as she loved her house and its beautiful setting, she missed being in her small bungalow in town. She could meet friends for lunch or dinner after a short ride or walk. Even if she didn't meet anyone, she could go out for coffee or pizza by herself.

Uncle Benjamin kept her company, when he chose to present himself. Tonight he had floated upstairs when they got home. He'd taken to sitting in his old room a lot. Franklin had asked her if she wanted help repainting it so she could move into the larger bedroom, but she'd declined. It felt as if Uncle Benjamin needed his own space.

She warmed up a frozen dinner of tilapia and peas, adding a roll and glass of white wine. She rarely watched television, but three weeks ago she and Franklin had placed a large antenna on the roof, so they could get broadcast channels. Franklin, used to Washington DC's instant news, missed being in the know.

Tonight she carried her dinner into the living room and turned on the Pittsburgh channel most likely to have news of Garrett County. After only a minute, Nellie Porter's face flashed on the screen. Digger could tell from the pastel blue loveseat that she was in Maryann's apartment. Her relaxed smile gave no hint of what would befall her.

A solemn-faced woman no older than Digger presented the story. "There are still no leads in the death of ninety-two-year-old Nellie Porter of Oakland, Maryland. People in the Garrett County seat expressed shock that anyone would harm the woman, who was well-liked at the Quiet Spring senior living complex."

The screen showed an outside view of the four-story building, and someone who looked like a manager refusing entry to a TV crew. "Ironically, Miss Porter long ago worked at the Mountain Granite Quarry, near Maple Grove, at the same time that Daniel Stevens did. His body was recently found buried near the town's old train depot."

Digger held her breath. She didn't want to hear her name.

The newscaster continued, "Just last week, Miss Porter wrote a letter critical of the Sheriff Department in 1963, which she believed should have worked much harder to learn what had happened to Mr. Stevens. Current sheriff, Roger Montgomery, said leads are sparse and asked for the community's help." The phone number for the sheriff flashed at the bottom of the screen.

The screen changed to a fresh-faced weather forecaster who told folks in the Appalachian Mountains to expect snow next week.

Digger finished her dinner and carried her dishes to the kitchen. She fed Bitsy and Ragdoll. The German Shepherd sat two feet from the cat, just far enough away not to be swatted, and watched his feline compatriot eat.

"You are such an optimist, Bitsy. She will never share her food with you."

Digger's cell phone rang, and she glanced at the caller ID. "Hello, Brian."

"Hi. Do you watch the local news?"

"Yes, I just saw the story. How is your great aunt doing?"

"She's really upset. She thinks if she hadn't been so angry about her brother that Nellie wouldn't have written that letter, and she might not have been killed."

"Does she truly think it was someone deliberately attacking Nellie?"

"Yes. Mom and Dad have gone down there to see her, but Dad had chemo today, so he won't be able to go again for a couple days. I guess I should."

His words hung in the air until Digger got his point. "Was that an invitation to join you?"

Brian almost gushed, "Would you?"

CHAPTER NINETEEN

DIGGER WOKE UP ON TUESDAY not looking forward to joining Brian later in the day as he visited Maryann Stevens. Nellie Porter's death weighed on her far more than that of Maryann's brother, but she could do nothing about it. Finding Daniel Stevens was hard, but he died long ago and she never met him. Before she found him, anyway. She willed herself to stop thinking so much about the two deaths.

She decided she'd pay attention, talk to Marty if he wanted a sounding board for his articles, and do her real job. She wouldn't risk her friendship with Holly by actively looking for information about either death.

As she prepared to leave, Bitsy sat at the front door with his stuffed lamb in his mouth.

"You silly boy. What would you do in a small office all day?"

Uncle Benjamin came up behind her. *"Bring him. He can sit near me."*

Holly wouldn't mind. Digger didn't want to argue with Bitsy and her uncle, who probably had not expected Bitsy to commandeer the front seat.

The promise of a forty-degree day meant Digger could take Bitsy for a couple of short walks. She remembered the photos of the depot ordered for Marilyn and Leon had come in the mail yesterday. Usually she would drive over to Frostburg to get the eight-by-tens, but mountain weather was so fickle she'd decided to have them mailed.

She could drive the photos to the quarry.

"I smell rubber burning."

"What? In the car?"

"Heh, heh. I can tell you're thinking about something."

"Oh, you. Do you think someone at the quarry killed Daniel Stevens?"

Uncle Benjamin was quiet for ten seconds. *"It's natural to suspect someone he knew. If a stranger tried to rob him or steal his car, his body or car would probably have been found. Someone had all the time in the world to dispose of him."*

"And his car. The Jones' place in Bloomington was on the edge of town. Back then, anyway."

"Hard to bury a car. I figure whoever did it kept it hidden for a time, then repainted it and drove it out of town. Lots of people have unattached garages, and it was cold."

"What does that have to do with anything?"

"What happens to a dead field mouse behind your refrigerator?"

"Ugh. So it should have been just as hard to hide Daniel's body until spring?"

"They could have put it in an outbuilding on the property. Maybe a standing freezer."

"Cheery thoughts." Digger pulled into a parking space in front of You Think, We Design. She fastened Bitsy's leash to his collar and made her way to the second floor. Bitsy had only been here one other time, and thought he should inspect every step. She disagreed and gave him a couple light tugs on his leash.

Holly had made coffee and had her mug to her lips. "You brought my boyfriend."

"That's a sad commentary."

"I did. I'm going to drive those photos to the quarry and figured he'd enjoy the ride."

Holly raised her eyebrows. "Looking for something up there?"

"Nope. I might ask to look at some of the annual reports from the early years. Maybe we can design something retro, or a combination of old and new."

"That could be a fun project."

WHEN DIGGER LEFT THE office at eleven, Bitsy again hogged the front seat of the Jeep.

"I've decided I'm not in favor of him coming to work with us."

"Can we leave anyone else at home?"

"I thought of a good way to spend my time."

"That's terrific!" Digger turned toward the west end of town so she could drive up the opposite side of the mountain from the Ancestral Sanctuary.

"But you have to help me."

"I should have known there'd be a catch."

"We go to the library, and I tell you what books to take out."

"Okay. But not today. I have a lot to do."

"I'll try not to sulk. So, why are we really making a hand delivery of these pictures?"

"I'm not sure why. I'm trying not to think about them, but it feels as if I should have some ideas about who killed them. Or at least Nellie."

Uncle Benjamin said nothing.

The parking lot at the quarry office had slush, left over from a one-inch snowfall the night before. They'd only had flurries on the east side of the mountain. Digger stomped her feet on the outside mat before going in.

The receptionist recognized her. "What brings you out today?"

"I took some photos at the depot the week before last, and Marilyn picked out several she wanted." Digger held up one envelope. "And I promised Leon a couple for this year's annual report, since you'll probably redo the gravel again."

The receptionist's eye's widened.

Digger glanced at her name plate. "What's up, Jennifer?"

"Oh, nothing. I'll call Marilyn. Have a seat."

Instead, Digger went to the photo of Daniel and Harlan that hung on the wall opposite the receptionist. She'd noticed it before, but never really studied it. Judging from the ages of the two men, the photo was taken years before Daniel's death.

"What's that they're standing on?"

Digger whispered "hot damn" as Marilyn walked into the reception area.

"What did you say?"

Digger turned. "The only photos I've seen of either your grandfather or Mr. Stevens have been in the paper, and they were taken when they were older. They look so…vibrant in that photo."

THE UNSCHEDULED MURDER TRIP

Marilyn stood next to her. "There aren't many pictures of them together."

"Makes sense." Digger smiled briefly. "They were in business long before people took pictures of everything they did."

"Speaking of photos, you have some for me?" She held out her hand.

"Yes, and for your father. I promised him I'd donate one for the annual report, no charge. Your invoice is in your envelope. No rush."

Marilyn glanced at the receptionist and turned to Digger. "Come on back to my office."

"Sure." As she followed the woman, Digger tried to picture the red carpet Daniel had been rolled in. It had been only about three feet wide, and no longer than his body. Of course, it could have been cut from a larger piece. She thought the carpet runner Daniel and Leon stood on in the picture had the same pattern. Since it was a black and white photo, she couldn't tell.

When they entered Marilyn's small office, she shut the door. Digger glanced around. Other parts of the business had older metal desks and file cabinets. Marilyn's was wood, as was the credenza behind it. Instead of merely blinds at the single window, she had a long, burgundy curtain.

"Looks cozy," Digger said.

"Looks expensive. I'm going to look around." Uncle Benjamin floated through the door.

Marilyn gestured to a chair. "Thanks. I told Dad that I needed a space that looked more professional than a factory floor."

"I get that." Digger waited for her to say more.

Marilyn walked behind her desk and sat. "I'm sorry you had to hear my grandmother and Mrs. Stevens shouting at each other."

"It happens. And they both had to feel pretty raw about finding Daniel. I met with Matthew Stevens a few nights ago, and he mentioned that his family used to go down to Bloomington when they fished. He said Isabella made butter and your grandmother made bread."

She smiled slightly. "I never heard that. Perhaps I'll tell Grandmother Mr. Stevens has good memories."

"I feel bad for Maryann and your grandmother. Felicia, isn't it?"

Marilyn nodded.

"Actually, everyone there. Imagine, having a neighbor murdered in their building."

She took a letter opener from a drawer to get to the pictures Digger had brought. "Yes, everyone is very upset. Especially because it happened in the daytime. Grandmother said they've all been told to lock their doors."

"I guess I understand why daytime should feel safe."

Marilyn examined each photo. "Thanks. I'll give the others to Dad." She shook her head. "I was so angry at Nellie Porter. I wanted it to…go away, and she wanted to spout her theory that Mr. Stevens had been here the night he went missing."

Digger looked at her and looked away.

Marilyn flushed. "I shouldn't have said it like that." She stood.

Digger understood that she'd been dismissed. "Call if you need other photos taken. I could go to one of your job sites." She grinned. "Our rates are very cheap for our best customer."

"Thanks. I'll let you find your way out."

Digger had no idea where Uncle Benjamin had gone. She hoped he realized she was leaving. She couldn't exactly loiter in the quarry parking lot.

Bitsy barked, loudly, several times. He didn't seem to like being alone in the car in an unfamiliar place.

Uncle Benjamin came through a window at the opposite end of the building. He slid into the back seat. *"Good thing Bitsy barked. You could have left me!"*

"I wouldn't. But I couldn't hang around in there for no reason. We'll have to come up with some sort of system so you'll know if I'm leaving a place."

"Move over, Dog." Uncle Benjamin squeezed into the front seat.

Bitsy whined.

"It's okay, boy. Your lamb's in the back. Go find it."

Bitsy climbed through Uncle Benjamin and settled on the back seat.

"There's something odd about that place, but I can't put my finger on it."

"You don't have a finger."

THE UNSCHEDULED MURDER TRIP

"It's an expression. I'm new at all this, but it almost felt as if there was some other being in there."

"You're giving me the heebie jeebies." Digger glanced sideways at her uncle. "If I didn't know you better, I'd say you're scared."

"Maybe I am. I just had a sense of something very dark. But I don't know what it means."

"Did you look at that picture of Daniel Stevens and Harlan Jones on the wall?"

"No."

"I thought the rug looked familiar."

"So, maybe the feeling means murder."

"Marilyn invited me back to her office. I felt as if she wanted to ask me something, but she didn't. She said everyone at Quiet Spring is locking their doors."

"After the horse is out of the barn."

CHAPTER TWENTY

DIGGER LEFT THE OFFICE at three Tuesday afternoon. She drove quickly up to the Ancestral Sanctuary to drop off Bitsy and Uncle Benjamin. He said he wouldn't mind prowling around Maryann's building, but Digger would be better at consoling her. All Bitsy cared about was that Digger put food in his bowl.

She picked up Brian at his parents' place by three-forty-five. Sylvia waved from the front door as she pulled it shut.

Brian slid into the passenger seat. "My parents really appreciated you going with me. I like Aunt Maryann, but I'm not sure how she'll be."

"No problem." Digger drove down Main Street, toward the highway. "Have you seen her since her friend Nellie died?"

"I've talked to her. I told her I had to finish two papers for school, and I'd be down soon."

"How do your parents think she's doing?"

"Not great. Her granddaughter was there, but she had to get back to Frostburg to be with her kids."

"I just realized, I don't know if her children are still alive."

"She had one son, Sheriff Montgomery's father, and he died a long time ago. She seems close to the sheriff and his sister. Florence, I think her name is."

Rain that would soon turn to sleet or freezing rain began to come down lightly. Digger didn't look forward to driving home from Oakland.

Talking to someone she didn't know well did not come easily to Digger. She turned the topic to a general discussion of how to do family history research, so time passed more quickly than if she'd asked about his studies.

THE UNSCHEDULED MURDER TRIP

Dusk greeted them in Oakland. A harried-looking woman about forty-five sat at a table by the front door of the Quiet Spring senior complex.

She greeted them with skepticism. "We're trying to be careful about who comes in."

"I get that," Digger said. She tilted her head to Brian. "Mrs. Stevens asked her great nephew to come down this evening."

The woman appeared relieved. "Good. She's been having us deliver meals to her room. See if you can encourage her to socialize more tomorrow."

"Yes, ma'am," Brian said, and led the way to Maryann's apartment.

She asked who it was before opening the door and, despite health guidance to do otherwise, hugged Brian. "Thank you both so much for coming."

"I believe I'm the official tea-maker. Should I get some for us?"

"A good idea, Digger. My dinner comes at five-thirty, but that's a ways away."

Brian walked with her toward the loveseat. "Do you usually eat in your apartment?"

Digger listened to them as she put mugs in the microwave and got teabags ready. Brian tried to keep the conversation light, but Maryann moved right to Nellie.

"I feel as if she would be alive if I hadn't talked to her so much about how angry I am that it took this long to find Daniel."

"I didn't know her," Brian said, "but from the letter she wrote to the paper, it didn't seem she had difficulty giving her own thoughts."

Maryann laughed lightly. "No one could say either of us was shy."

Digger carried two of the mugs to the coffee table and went back for her own. "I haven't seen anything on the news about whether the sheriff's office has made progress."

"Roger said the security cameras don't cover every part of the hallways. I remember a lot of people objected to what one man called 'close surveillance.' People are rethinking that now."

"So they can't see if anyone entered her apartment that morning?" Digger asked.

"No. Other people were in the hall, but no one recalled seeing her open her door to anyone."

"Do visitors have to sign in?" Brian asked.

Maryann shook her head. "Residents have to sign out, so they know where we are, but it's assisted living, not a nursing home. Guests can come and go until the doors are locked at eight PM. Then they ring a doorbell."

After a few minutes of trivial conversation, Digger's cell phone rang. Marty's name appeared. "If you don't mind, I'll step into the hall and take this."

She shut the door behind her as she pressed the answer button. "What's up?"

"Is that your car in the apartment lot?"

"You mean with the bumper sticker that asks if you've hugged your family tree today?"

"Yep, that one. Are you with Maryann?"

"I drove down with Brian. His parents came yesterday, but his dad had chemo today."

"Digger, can you ask her a couple questions for me?"

"When did you get shy?"

"Never happen," Marty said. "They know who I am, so they don't let me in."

"What do you want to know?"

"Whether Felicia Jones can walk well enough to get into Nellie Porter's apartment and push her down."

"I've only seen her pushed in a wheelchair, but I can vouch for her not seeing well. Her eyes are fogged from cataracts."

"Huh. I checked out Marilyn Jones…Davis. She drives a pink Cadillac SUV. Pretty noticeable anywhere, but especially in Garrett County."

"And has anyone seen her?"

"That's the funny part," Marty said. "She's been around every day for the last four or five. She told staff at the Quiet Spring that she wanted to spend time with her grandmother, because she'd been upset about the discovery of Daniel Stevens' body."

"If you can't get in here, how do you know that?"

"Woman I talked to at the gas station. The one on the way out of town. She works at the place, and apparently the staff are real skittish."

"I'm surprised she confided in you."

"She came up to me. She'd seen the lady at the door throw me out, and she wanted to know what I knew."

Digger thought about that. "If I were plotting something, I'd try to get people used to seeing me in a place, so they wouldn't pay much attention to me."

"So, how's Maryann?"

"Guilty. She thinks Nellie wouldn't have spouted off if Maryann hadn't been angry. If she hadn't written that letter to the editor or confronted Felicia, maybe she'd be alive."

A staff member came down the hall toward Digger, who nodded and stood closer to the wall. To Marty, she said, "Just a sec."

"You okay?"

"Yep." She lowered her voice. "Just waiting for someone to walk by. You think Nellie's death was an accident?"

"Makes some sense. Broad daylight, no weapon."

Digger remembered Uncle Benjamin saying a chair had been overturned. "Any sign of a struggle?"

"Haven't heard of any." He sighed. "Usually a deputy will tell me something. One of them said the sheriff told them to zip it this time. Probably because his grandmother lives there."

"So where does that leave you?" Digger asked.

"I notice you didn't say 'us.'"

She smiled. "I can't look overtly. If for no other reason, Holly would kill me."

"Okay. Keep your eyes open."

"I already am. I'll call you tomorrow."

When Digger reentered the apartment, she saw a look of almost desperation on Brian's face. "I didn't mean to step out for so long."

Maryann didn't hide a conspiratorial look. "That reporter friend of yours?"

"Yes. He's trying to…figure out what went on, too."

Maryann shook her head. "I think Felicia sent someone to talk to Nellie, and it went beyond conversation."

"Why do you say that?" Brian asked.

"Do you mean someone from her family?" Digger asked.

"Maybe, but Felicia thinks she's the queen bee. And she tips the staff. We aren't supposed to do that. So, if she asked a staff member to talk to Nellie, a couple of them would do it."

"Why?" Brian repeated.

Maryann shrugged. "I think she wanted Nellie to shut up, and she couldn't go to her apartment on her own. Nellie could be a hot-head sometimes. She wouldn't have taken kindly to any suggestion."

Brian shifted in his chair.

"Gosh," Digger said. "We came down here to cheer you up, and look what we're talking about."

"It's all I think about," Maryann said.

DIGGER LOOKED FOR MARTY as she and Brian left the Quiet Spring, but didn't see him. A subdued Brian said little, and because of a light rain-snow mix, Digger paid close attention to her driving.

"You okay?" she finally asked.

"Yeah. I guess I had myself convinced that her friend's death was an accident. She really doesn't think so."

When he said nothing, Digger said, "I probably shouldn't have talked to her about it."

"She wanted to talk. Do you know what kind of investigation they're doing?"

"Sheriff Montgomery is a straight shooter, and Maryann is his grandmother. Even if he doesn't have a lot to go on, he'll keep looking."

Brian nodded. "If I were in his shoes, I'd be afraid to stop."

CHAPTER TWENTY-ONE

DIGGER WORKED STEADILY WEDNESDAY morning. She finished designing new letterhead for a local law firm and drafted the layout for the Mountain Granite Quarry annual report. She had tried keeping the same design theme as their new brochure, and thought it worked.

She brought the design up on her largest computer screen. "What do you think?"

Holly studied it. "I like the bold lines. You think they'll want the blue and gold?"

Digger tapped a key and a red and dark gray color scheme appeared. "They can choose. Or pick something else."

"You just want to go out there and snoop."

"A bit. Mostly I want to see if the sheriff is in his satellite office and stop by."

Holly raised her eyebrows.

"That rug he was…in. It kind of looks like one in a photo in the quarry admin office."

"Don't you think the sheriff can figure that out?"

Digger shrugged. "Maybe, but why would he study that photo on the wall? It doesn't relate to the murder."

"Don't get yourself killed."

DIGGER SAT OUTSIDE THE sheriff's Maple Grove office. He'd said he'd see her, but she thought he might be keeping her waiting on purpose.

After another five minutes, he opened his door and gestured she should enter. "What's up, Digger?"

"There's this picture on the wall in the quarry office, and…"

"What were you doing out there?

"I work for them. I dropped off some photos."

He acknowledged he'd interrupted her with a nod. "Go on."

"I've looked at it before, but this time I studied it more. I'd never paid that much attention to Daniel Stevens. The thing is, he and Harlan Jones seem to be standing on a runner."

"What do you mean a runner?"

Digger smiled. "Carpet runner. Like you might have by a front door or as an accent rug."

Sheriff Montgomery appeared amused. "I'm not too familiar with accent rugs."

Digger's smile faded. "It looks like the pattern. Of the rug…you know."

He sat up straighter. "That's a strong thing to say."

"It would be if I were accusing someone of murder. All I'm doing is suggesting you might ask for a copy of the photograph to compare to the carpet he was," she cleared her throat, "rolled in."

"Huh. I saw that picture when I went out there to talk to Leon. I'll have to take another look."

"Now, can I ask you something?"

"This isn't tit for tat, Digger."

"I know. I read all the newspaper articles from when Daniel disappeared. They talk about Harlan helping with the search, even going to the office to see if he was there. But I didn't find anything that accounted for his time. And his wife's."

"Digger."

She thought she was about to be asked to leave, so she pressed on. "And that bartender who saw Daniel. Is he still alive?"

"He is, and he has nothing to add to what he told one of my predecessors fifty-odd years ago." He pointed to the door.

"Okay, I just wanted to make sure you knew that Marilyn Jones, Marilyn Davis, has been visiting her grandmother a lot lately."

He almost smiled. "Old-time newspapers used to have columns to say who visited whoever."

"I know, but…"

Sheriff Montgomery held up a hand. "Enough. We are talking to anyone who was in the Quiet Spring complex for the last two weeks. Now you need to let me do my job."

THE UNSCHEDULED MURDER TRIP

Digger stood, but turned back at the door. "I never saw how Mr. Stevens died."

"Cracked skull. Be in the paper this week."

She sat in her car for several minutes. She had a good reason to go up to the quarry offices. Could she risk alienating a good client by talking about the murder of one of the company's founders?

She decided she could judge Leon Jones' mood and go from there.

She called Marty as she drove to the quarry. "I looked harder at a picture in the quarry office. The rug Daniel Stevens and Harlan Jones are standing on looks like the one Daniel was wrapped in for 50-plus years."

He did a low whistle. "Sheriff Montgomery said he'd talk to me more about the initial autopsy report. I'll ask about what they've found out about that disintegrating carpet and see where that goes."

As the receptionist led her to Leon's office, Digger glanced into Marilyn's and saw her back was to the door as she spoke on the phone. Her father's office contrasted with her wooden furniture and burgundy curtain.

Leon Jones had a large, gray metal desk. She bet it weighed at least eighty pounds. He had arrayed eight or ten folders, each labeled with a company name, across the top of the desk. Leon stood and extended a hand. Then he noted Digger's mask and withdrew the hand and pulled up his own.

"The hardest time for me to remember is when I'm in the office. It feels so normal here."

She nodded. "Holly and I talk about that. We're together so much, we usually don't have them on when we're alone, but always with clients." She slid her oversized, leather folder to him. "And here is what we have for one of our favorite clients."

Jones opened the folder and his face brightened. "Very interesting. So each page of text would have these borders, right?"

"Yes. You can pick the colors. You could alternate, but most firms want to plant an image in customers' minds, so they try to adhere to a theme."

As their conversation wound down, Digger moved to houses. "You know I inherited Uncle Benjamin's place, the Ancestral Sanctuary."

"I do. Quite a lot to maintain."

She nodded and smiled. "I was actually going to talk to you about that. I think it's about the same size as your parents' old place and…"

He stiffened slightly. "You've seen that house in Bloomington?"

She nodded. "I've taken photos all over the county. You saw me at the depot."

He relaxed. "Of course."

"I like anything old. But, it's going to be hard for me to choose what to best maintain."

He frowned.

"I know, gutters and downspouts help keep water away from the foundation, if you don't keep the roof in good repair the house'll be gone in a generation. But what would you say the next couple of things are? To be sure I do, I mean."

"Hmm. My parents built that house before I was born, but not by much. About 1960 or thereabouts, so it probably had fewer upkeep requirements. Except for the damn cellar. It shouldn't have been built in that dip." He saw her puzzled express. "Kind of at the foot of a hill."

"Oh. Did your basement flood?"

"Not so much flooding as a high water table. We weren't that far from the river. A lot of melting snow made dampness, water even, rise up from the soil into the concrete."

"Ugh. I'm higher up a mountain, so that's not an issue. Mostly just lots of little things. Exterior paint, creaky porch railings. The usual with old houses." She stood. "Let us know what color schemes you want."

Marilyn appeared in the doorway. "Color schemes for what?"

Digger nodded at the folder on Leon's desk. "Your annual report."

"Oh." She looked at her father. "Do I get input?"

"As long as it doesn't involve mauve."

THE UNSCHEDULED MURDER TRIP

He said it in a teasing tone, but Digger figured he didn't like some of Marilyn's ideas that he saw as more feminine.

Digger tried to make her tone sympathetic. "How's your grandmother doing?"

"My mother?" Leon asked.

"I've seen Marilyn down there when I'm been visiting Maryann Stevens. Montgomery."

Leon said, "Just fine."

Marilyn said, "Still upset about Ms. Porter's death."

"Ah," Leon said. "I didn't get what you meant. Very sad."

"I go down to visit Maryann a couple times a week, for now. Sheriff Montgomery seems certain he'll find out what happened. Even if it was an accident, somebody needs to be accountable."

"Very true." Leon stood up. "I'll get back to you in a day or two."

Digger wasn't sure if it was her imagination or if Marilyn really looked stricken.

AS SHE DROVE BACK TO TOWN, Digger considered what else might be on the Jones property. She knew the county plat book, which showed what was on land as well as who owned it, had been placed online years ago. She didn't want to drive down to Oakland to look at the plat for the Jones' parcel, so she went online back at the office.

Uncle Benjamin sat on a four-drawer file cabinet. *"About time you came back."*

Digger glanced at the door and didn't see Holly. She hung her coat on the rack by the door. "You could've come."

"The place had a dark vibe."

"I have some computer work to do. Have you been in the attic lately?"

Uncle Benjamin vanished without a goodbye.

After she'd looked at the various parcels near Bloomington, she realized that since the Jones hadn't owned the land for years, their name wouldn't be associated with it. That led her on a search to see if she could find the location by calling the county zoning office.

She knew that many older phone books had been scanned and were online. Sure enough Jones, H. and F. had a listing in the 1962 Bloomington phone directory. The 32-page document had been produced by local merchants rather than a phone company. She considered herself lucky.

A call to the zoning office told her which plat went with that address, and she pulled it up online. She zoomed in. A bank in North Carolina owned the property.

"That's handy."

She hadn't learned much, though she could see a narrow road still led to it. No way to tell if it was private or not. She didn't feel she'd learned enough to make it worth her time, but no way to tell that in advance. Holly returned from lunch just after Digger printed the portion of the plat that had the Jones' old property.

"What did Leon Jones think of the design?"

"He liked it. He hasn't picked colors yet."

MARTY CALLED DIGGER AT home at seven-thirty. He sounded good-natured. "I'll share if you will."

"Share what?

"Marilyn Jones Davis confessed to accidentally causing Nellie Porter to fall and hit her head. Or, as we say in the real world, sounds like she killed her and wished she didn't."

"My God. I saw her today."

"I know. She said, and I quote, "Digger Browning's devotion to my grandfather's partner's sister, Maryann Stevens, gave me the courage to come forward."

"I think I'm going to throw up."

"Yeah, Sheriff Montgomery kind of looked like he wanted to."

CHAPTER TWENTY-TWO

FRIDAY'S *MAPLE GROVE NEWS* was not as kind to Marilyn Jones Davis as the Pittsburgh media had been. The story depicted her as a young woman of privilege who concerned herself a great deal with her image.

Rather than say that she and her husband had come to Maple Grove because of job losses and the chance for her to participate in the family business, Marty had dug into her prior career as an event planner. Yes, the industry spiraled when the country went into lockdown, but her firm (Marilyn's Meetings and More) had struggled before that. She was lucky to have a family business to go to.

In contrast, her husband – who had joined every service club since moving to Maple Grove – was portrayed as an innovative entrepreneur with the public relations firm he'd founded. And very supportive of his wife.

Uncle Benjamin had been reading over Digger's shoulder. *"The word skewered comes to mind."*

"I'll say. By the time they get to her little 'shove' of Nellie, she comes across as a selfish witch."

Marilyn said she visited Nellie to ask her to stop spreading rumors about the Jones family and their business. She suggested that Nellie had been rude. When Marilyn turned to leave, Nellie grabbed her arm. Marilyn yanked her arm away and Nellie lost her balance and tripped over her own dining room chair. She flailed backward hard, and hit the corner of the counter between the kitchen and dining area.

"I don't believe a word of it."

"It doesn't say if she even tried to help. She's a child of privilege who grew into an adult with a strong sense of entitlement."

ELAINE L. ORR

Sheriff Montgomery had said he was looking into all aspects of the tragic death, and Marilyn was released on her own recognizance because of her strong ties to the community.

Marty called ten minutes later, as Digger finished her coffee. "What do you think?"

Uncle Benjamin glided over to listen.

"Fair. I thought the TV station in Pittsburgh acted as if poor Marilyn was the victim."

"She can really lay on the charm."

"How come you didn't have a quote from Maryann?"

Marty half-snorted. "None of it was printable."

"Go Maryann!" Uncle Benjamin went back to an article about the upcoming Pittsburgh Steelers game.

"So, Digger, does her confession bring any closure for you?"

"No. Nellie's insistence that Daniel was in the quarry offices the night he vanished, well, died, must have worried the Jones family. Or at least Marilyn. They know something."

"Damn. Persistence is your middle name. What the heck else can you do?"

"Remember how Daniel went to a bar that night?"

"Yeah, the Crow's Nest. Gone now."

"But the bartender's still alive," Digger said. "Do you know his name?"

"Where is he? A nursing home or something?"

"He lives with his daughter, but I don't know his name, or hers."

Marty didn't say anything.

"You know, don't you?"

"Harrison Hunter. I didn't think he was alive, much less had a daughter. How do you know this?"

"I asked the sheriff. The guy isn't well, and didn't want to talk. His daughter told Montgomery he didn't have more to add."

Marty raised an eyebrow. "So you think he'll talk to you?"

"I can be charming."

"You should take me. I can give you tips."

Marty said nothing.

"Come on. Can you find out his daughter's name?"

THE UNSCHEDULED MURDER TRIP

AT THREE-THIRTY, DIGGER knocked on the door of Alice Beckett, the widowed daughter of Harrison Hunter. She would have called, but the phone number was unlisted. She carried a loaf of banana bread from the Mountain Edge Bakery.

A woman about fifty opened the door. Her expression did not welcome a visitor.

"Hi. I'm Digger Browning. I'm a friend of Maryann Stevens." She held up the banana bread. "I'd trade you and your father a loaf of banana bread for ten minutes of his time."

She opened the door. "That's a good technique. You can come in for a minute, but it's not likely he'll talk to you."

Digger stepped into the entry foyer and handed the bread to Alice, who regarded her solemnly. "I'm sorry you had to be the one to find Daniel Stevens."

"Me, too. Though in some ways, it helped his sister. She never believed he deserted his family."

Alice gestured to a stuffed chair near the door. "Have a seat." She headed for a hallway off the living room.

Digger took in the space. The house was a typical mountain bungalow, probably built in the 1930s or 1940s. The neat room was not well appointed. The deep blue slipcovers on the couch looked worn, and the only decoration was a silk flower wreath in Thanksgiving colors.

Alice returned, smiling. "I'm amazed. He'd like to talk to you. I think it was the banana bread." She pointed toward the hall. "Second room on the left."

An alert-looking man who seemed close to eighty sat in a recliner with a television nearby. The small room held a single bed, dresser, a straight-backed chair, and an overflowing bookcase. The walls were adorned with Pittsburgh Pirates pennants.

"Hi. Thanks for talking to me."

"I didn't want to talk to the sheriff, but I do have something to say. Have a seat."

Digger sat. "Thanks."

With a slightly shaking hand, he lifted a cup of water and took a sip. "You probably read the papers. I guess I was the last one saw Daniel. Well, besides his killer."

She nodded. "It didn't seem that you spoke to him much."

"Hardly at all. He was reading a piece of paper, so I left him alone." He drew a breath. "The other person who came in, maybe half-an-hour later, was Harlan Jones."

Digger's eyes widened. "I didn't know that."

"Nobody alive would remember. Didn't give it much thought. He said he and his wife were spending the night at the Land Grant Inn, because of the snow. He ordered a gin and tonic."

Harrison Hunter took another sip of water. "He drank it pretty fast, and left a big tip. Then he motioned I should come over, and said his drink was on the QT. He'd told his wife he was swearing off the stuff."

Digger wet her lips. "But you didn't think it related to Daniel, so you didn't initially mention it to the deputies."

"I didn't even think about it. To be honest, I was known to take a nip or two back then. Wasn't supposed to when I worked the bar."

"I can see why it would seem innocuous," Digger said.

"In the paper a few days later, it said Harlan Jones offered a $5,000 reward to anyone who could lead them to Daniel. That's when I realized I maybe should have told the sheriff and his guys."

"But you'd waited, so it didn't seem like a good idea."

"Yeah. Sheriff back then was a rude sot. Sheriff Blackman. He would have given me a ration, maybe even made me go down to his office to talk about it. Everybody'd think I was a suspect."

Digger nodded slowly. "And Harlan was Daniel's friend and business partner. He wasn't…breaking any laws by having a drink."

"No, but I always wondered if he had another reason to want me to keep mum. I should've told the sheriff, but after a few days, I just couldn't."

DIGGER FINALLY GOT HOLD of Marty about seven-thirty that evening. "Wait until you hear this." She relayed what Harrison Hunter had said.

THE UNSCHEDULED MURDER TRIP

"Huh, banana bread. I'll have to try that."

"That's not the point."

"I know, relax. Just trying to think where to go with this."

"I think that Harlan figured if Daniel wasn't at the Knights of Columbus or the bar, he went to the office. And Harlan had things he wanted to hide. He was the embezzler. That's how they had that big house." Digger drew a breath.

"You could be in the Olympics if they had a sport for jumping to conclusions."

"Come on, Marty. I'm serious."

"I can tell. And I'm going to figure out what to do next. We can't just head over to Mountain Granite Quarry and ask Leon if he thinks his father killed his partner."

"Maybe you can't, but I could."

"You…could. I don't think it would get you anything but thrown out of his office. I'm a journalist. I have to start with facts. Or at least a semblance of them."

"We have a starting point!"

"Digger, sometimes you have to know when to back off."

"I'm not good at that."

"No kidding."

Digger pushed the off button on her phone. When she turned around, Uncle Benjamin hovered only a foot from her.

"You sure you want to end a conversation like that?"

"I can't stand to be patronized."

"You also can't stand to lose a good friend."

CHAPTER TWENTY-THREE

DIGGER WOKE SUNDAY MORNING feeling frustrated, or maybe it was defeated. It seemed that Marilyn Jones Davis would not face charges, at least initially, in Nellie Porter's so-called accidental death. Who in their right mind would believe Nellie tripped over her chair while Marilyn happened to be standing there?

Ragdoll jumped on her head and placed a paw on Digger's nose. "I'm going back to sleep."

Bitsy barked from her blanket in the corner.

"Apparently I'm not."

She stumbled around the kitchen and almost put cat food in Bitsy's bowl. "Are you around?"

"Right behind you, cuz."

Digger dropped the bowl of water she'd been about to place next to Bitsy's food. "Franklin, I didn't hear you."

"I thought you heard me come downstairs earlier today. You said something when I walked by your door."

"Oh, right. Did I tell you I went to bed early?"

He eyed her. "I know you've had a rough week, but are you all right?"

She tried to make her smile look mildly cheerful. "Right as rain."

Franklin raised his eyebrows. "I'm going to drive down to Maple Grove and buy us breakfast sandwiches at that new diner on Main Street."

"That'd be great. I'll be fully functional when you get back."

"Seeing's believing."

Digger grabbed a dish towel to mop the floor. When she finished, she leaned against the kitchen sink. "Why do I care about this so much?"

THE UNSCHEDULED MURDER TRIP

Uncle Benjamin appeared on the kitchen table and Ragdoll jumped up to join him. *"Because you don't want to see a killer go free."*

"It isn't just one. I'd bet anything her grandmother told her something about Daniel Stevens. Where were you, anyway?"

"Watching my son make some notes in his diary."

"Oh. Wait. I found yours, yours and your father's, when I was getting familiar with the house months ago."

If a ghost could look uncomfortable, Uncle Benjamin did. *"I saw they were still hidden in the back of the top shelf in the linen closet. Didn't realize you found them."*

She grinned. "I didn't read them. Do you want Franklin to have them?"

"I might. I'll let you know."

"I'm going upstairs to shower." Digger turned toward the front staircase, but then looked back. "I thought of something a few days ago. If you find other spirits, will they come here?"

"Hadn't thought about it. Figured you'd take me for dates."

FRANKLIN'S SANDWICHES HIT THE spot, and he headed back to the attic to keep working. Digger finished drying her hair as her cell phone rang. She saw Marty's name and decided not to answer it. Then she thought she was being childish.

"Hello reporter with ethics."

He grunted a laugh. "I'm sorry I gave you a hard time."

"You were right. I jumped to conclusions."

"Could I hear that first part again?"

"Ha. Ha." She smiled in spite of herself and picked up a scrunchie for her hair and started for the steps.

"I'm rethinking part of my initial response," Marty said.

"Would that have been the part about me knowing when to butt out?"

"Tangential. You were talking about how the Jones' old house in Bloomington has been vacant for years."

Digger passed through the dining room where Uncle Benjamin and Ragdoll sat on the table. She scolded him with her finger. "I guess they sold it at some point…"

"After Harlan died, which was quite a while ago. It turned over several times, and the Great Recession tossed it into foreclosure."

Uncle Benjamin floated off the table, apparently keen to listen to her conversation.

Digger opened the fridge and took out a bottle of water. "Something Leon said made me think it had water problems."

"Which makes you wonder why his mother recently talked about buying it back."

"Where'd you hear that?" Digger asked.

"A guy who works at a gas station in Oakland, whose sister works at the Quiet Spring. In the kitchen."

"Why would he talk to you about that?"

"Because I told him I was a reporter and asked him what he thought about Nellie Porter's death."

"That was Marilyn, not Felicia."

"But apparently Felicia is rude to a lot of the staff, and this guy's sister hoped she'd move out."

"But she didn't." Digger thought for a moment. "I bet something's hidden in Bloomington."

"Sounds like a good point. We should go there."

Digger continued. "But someone lived in the property for many years after the Jones sold it. Wouldn't anything hidden have been found?"

"In the house, probably, but they had what, three acres?"

"Yes. It was on the edge of town." Digger didn't mention that she'd asked the county zoning office to tell her how to identify the plat information for that area.

"Right. And we know there was coal mined there, and the larger mines have been filled. But that area had some small mines. That's really too fancy a term."

"Small seams of coal on private property. People used it to heat their homes. But you can't do that now."

"Not since just after the Depression."

"Why would it matter if one was on the old Jones property?"

"Wonder what you could hide in one of those small mines?"

Digger thought for a moment. "A car, perhaps?"

THE UNSCHEDULED MURDER TRIP

THE SUN PEEKED THROUGH clouds as Digger climbed into Marty's Toyota and Uncle Benjamin floated through the back window.

Franklin waved from the front porch. "You have your key? I'll probably be gone when you get back."

Digger pulled it out of her pocket and waved it. Then she placed a cooler with sandwiches and freshly baked brownies next to Uncle Benjamin. "If you're on good behavior, I'll give you a brownie."

Marty smiled. "I'll do my best."

"Are you working on a second article about Nellie Porter's death?"

"Yep. I guess I don't want to believe it was an accident either, but I don't have a specific reason to argue with Sheriff Montgomery about it."

After half-an-hour, they crested a hill above Bloomington. Digger squinted. She could see the Potomac River less than a quarter-mile past the last houses. "River only has ice right by the shore."

"I haven't been down this way much. Does it ever freeze over?"

"Not often. I keep forgetting you've only lived here a few years. It ices up a lot, but not enough to walk on most years." She consulted her phone's navigation software. "Turn right in a couple hundred yards. Doesn't look like much of a road."

Marty turned slowly. "Looks like a former road. Almost a long driveway."

"A rutted driveway. Hope you have good tires."

"You know how to change one right? I taught you."

Digger inclined her head slightly.

They drove another few hundred yards down the so-called road, and then the house appeared on their left. It sat at the base of a small hill, and another rose behind it. Digger's eyes swept the property. "Kind of a little valley, isn't it?"

Marty put the car in park, and they stared at what had once been a beautiful, if secluded, residence. It had Victorian characteristics, but what might have once been charming now looked decidedly forlorn. In an attempt to either modernize or avoid painting a lot of old wood, someone had massacred the designer's intent by covering much of the house in vinyl siding.

Boards covered first-floor windows, but second-floor windows still had their glass. Grass in the area immediately around the house had apparently been mowed periodically, but beyond that, the acreage looked as it might have in pioneer days.

Like much of the area, the land featured rolling hills rather than tall peaks. Since it had never been farmed, protruding rocks remained. Several–some large enough to be called boulders–jutted from the ground.

Marty drove the car down the small hill and parked by the front porch.

Digger watched Uncle Benjamin float up to a second-floor window. She didn't expect him to enter, but he did just that.

"Do you see something up there?" Marty asked.

"I wonder why no one ever tried to break those windows?"

"Pretty high up. Need a pitcher's arm."

Digger frowned. "I wonder why no one bought it after the foreclosure?"

"Kind of gives new meaning to the word fixer-upper, don't you think?"

"I wouldn't want to tackle it," she said.

Uncle Benjamin came through the front door and waved to Digger. She caught herself before she waved back and instead gestured around the property. "You think we should start here and work out, or at the edge of the property and work in?"

"I'd say here and back. That way we aren't wading through the grass and sticks as much."

"There's some broken furniture still in there on the top floor, but it wouldn't have belonged to the Jones family."

"I've got a couple things in my trunk that we can use." He popped the trunk and pulled out a short and long pair of lawn clippers, two pair of work gloves, and a Maglite.

Digger pulled a short, but powerful, flashlight from her pocket. "Should have thought of clippers."

THE UNSCHEDULED MURDER TRIP

He grinned. "Too bad no one owns it. We could charge them for landscaping." He handed her the clippers. "I have one more thing."

Digger laughed as he drew out the long rod, shorter than a yard rake, with a round disc on the bottom. "A metal detector?"

"Sure. Cheap on Amazon. If they buried it in pieces, we might find it."

She stopped laughing. "Good idea."

They walked to the edge of the mowed area and looked beyond it. Uncle Benjamin floated off to the back of the property.

Digger tried to pay attention to him. "It seems as if it would be kind of hilly near a cave, don't you think?"

"I guess, but maybe you also had to climb into a small mine and there's wood over a hole."

"That's reassuring."

The hill that rose from the back of the house wasn't steep. They paced off squares of about twenty feet and walked them, but not together. As she tried to keep track of Uncle Benjamin, Digger almost tripped over a rock partially hidden in the grass.

She caught herself in time. "This is not a place to be if you need an ambulance."

"True. I have band aids in the car, but if you break a leg, they won't be much help." He moved the disc of the metal detector closer to the dirt. "I don't pick up anything."

"How deep can it detect?" Digger asked.

He grinned. "Not too deep."

At one point, the ground seemed soft, but closer examination made Digger think a family of moles had made themselves at home on the property.

Marty called to her from twenty yards away. "See anything? Oh, I have beeping." He stooped and pawed at the dirt with a finger. "Bottle cap."

Digger only half heard him. Up the small hill, almost where the property line would be, Uncle Benjamin waved both arms and gestured that Digger should come that way.

"What are you looking at?" Marty asked.

She improvised. "Something shiny. I wonder if it could be a lock covering an entrance."

Marty shielded his eyes. "Don't see it."

Uncle Benjamin did a mid-air somersault, so Digger knew he really wanted her up there. She began to climb the hill.

"Where are you going? Are you sure you see something?"

"No, but there's only one way to find out." She tried to keep Uncle Benjamin in her line of sight, but he dove to the ground and seemingly hid in the tall grass.

"So much for plans to work our way back gradually."

"I'm sorry, it feels important." Digger plowed ahead. As she neared the top of the hill, which would likely be the edge of the property, she saw what appeared to be roughly a six-by-nine-inch window in the ground. A pile of small rocks sat in front of it, and she had the impression they used to cover the window. She knelt next to it.

Marty joined her a few seconds later. "An entrance do you think?"

"Since it has a screen rather than glass, maybe it's for ventilation." She gingerly touched the screen and part of it disintegrated. "Must be really old."

Marty scraped the ground around the window with the handle of his clippers. "Wish I'd thought to bring a shovel." He stood. "Let's look for more of these little air holes, or whatever they are."

Digger put her face closer to the window and was rewarded with a pair of eyes staring back at her. "Good God!"

Marty turned quickly. "What is it?"

"A field mouse ran right across my hand."

"You and mice." He continued prowling the hillside.

Digger remembered she had used the mouse excuse when Uncle Benjamin had startled her in the library. She'd have to think of others. Or figure out better ways to ditch Uncle Benjamin as she left the house.

"Sorry. It's really neat down here. Cool and dark."

She was too close to Marty to respond to Uncle Benjamin. Then she thought of something. "Marty, you have that Maglite in your pocket?"

"Yep, what…oh, why didn't I think of that?" He came back and knelt next to Digger.

THE UNSCHEDULED MURDER TRIP

She moved a few inches away so he could get close enough to the window to peer into what lay below.

He put his face close to the window. "You wanted me to look in so your face didn't get filthy." He shone the light into the space below.

"See anything?"

Behind her, Uncle Benjamin chuckled. *"Just wait 'til you see what's down there."*

Marty sat up and passed her the light. "You're going to have to get dirty. It's a small area, and I see a pile of stuff against one wall."

She took the light and got so close her nose touched the screen. She pulled back a little and bounced the light's beam around the space. The pile of 'stuff' was not neatly stacked.

A hard-side suitcase leaned up against what seemed to be a jumble of old boards. Then she looked closer.

The car's pieces had retained some of their blue color, and the fins made it clear parts of an old Ford Fairlane had been buried on the Jones' property.

CHAPTER TWENTY-FOUR

DIGGER TURNED SLOWLY TO see Marty's mouth partially open. An expression of incredulity, she thought. He didn't even bother to push his glasses back up his nose.

She felt a mix of disbelief and relief. "They really did it. I mean, I thought it had to be one of the Jones, but they were friends. And Matthew seemed to remember them fondly." She stopped. "I'm babbling."

"You're entitled. I wouldn't have pursued this if you hadn't…"

Something hard hit Digger in the shoulder blades and she stumbled forward a step. At the same time, what sounded like a bunch of bees sped by behind her, and a loud noise seemed to echo.

Marty squatted and pulled her hand so hard she fell to the ground. "What was that?"

"I'm pretty sure it was a bullet."

Digger thought she heard a huge door being slammed, and dust rose from a spot behind her.

"Now I'm positive," Marty said. "Crawl!"

"They can't see us, the grass is too tall."

More bees roared past and dust spurted.

"They aren't aiming at seagulls!"

Marty was a lot bigger than she was, and he couldn't move as fast as Digger without rising above the grass. Digger could have passed him, but instead she lifted her head a few inches. "Those huge rocks. Ten yards head."

Digger had just put her head back down when a bullet whizzed over her head, roughly where her scalp had been. Marty rose to a crouch and yelled, "Run."

The rocks were only about eight yards away, but when Digger reached them her lungs burned as if she'd run a mile. A bullet pinged and dust drifted down.

"Are you crazy?" She squatted behind what she hoped was the rock's tallest point.

Marty leaned his back into the rock and slid down it, ending up in a sitting position. "Timing," he panted.

The sound of bullets stopped. Neither said anything for several seconds.

"What do you mean, timing?"

His breathing slowed. "I don't know a lot about rifles. But either that was an old one that needed to be cocked between each shot, or the shooter needed time to aim between each one."

Digger changed from squatting to sitting next to Marty, their shoulders touching. She shut her eyes briefly. Then they popped open and she stood. "My God! Uncle Benjamin!"

Marty yanked her hand and she fell back on her butt. "What the hell, Digger?"

But she'd seen all she needed to see. Uncle Benjamin lay on the ground, on his stomach, near where she and Marty had stood. She remembered him saying he wanted to be able to move items, but so far could not. It looked as if he'd finally been able to, and pushing Digger away had taken all his strength.

She thought she saw movement, but couldn't be sure. Could ghosts be killed a second time?

Marty was talking to her. "Digger, you can't stand up like that. Stay down."

"Right." Her heart pounded and a single tear ran down each cheek. She rubbed them away with one hand.

Tires screeched for a moment. Digger thought it was from the road, or at least farther down the rutted driveway, close to the road.

Marty pulled his phone from the pocket of his jeans and studied it. "No frigging signal. You?"

She reached into the pocket of her jacket and looked at her own. "No. Don't you think they left?"

"You want to stick your head up again and find out?"

"No thanks."

A heavy-sounding vehicle drove quickly down the drive. Digger popped her head up and down quickly. "Brown pick-up truck. Big. Not trying to hide."

They scrambled to their feet. A large man in a flannel shirt and hunting vest got out of the truck. A black long gun rested at his side, easily held in one hand.

"He's not the shooter," Marty said. "He raised a hand and waved. Up here."

"What the hell are you two doing? This is private property!"

Marty yelled. "Avoiding bullets. We're coming down."

More quietly, Digger said, "I'll be right behind you."

When Marty was several yards ahead of her, she knelt next to Uncle Benjamin. He was so transparent he appeared almost invisible. She whispered his name.

He turned his head to one side. *"I think I'll be okay. Go with Marty."*

"I can't leave you."

"Sure you can. Try to keep people from stepping on me, would you?"

AN HOUR LATER, DIGGER and Marty sat on the house's porch steps with the man they now knew as Samuel Blair, Digger in the middle. The sheriff had finished his initial questioning and told them to "stay the hell out of his way."

Digger turned her head to Samuel. "How did you know the shots came from up here?"

His deeply lined face confirmed Blair had been a smoker, and his husky voice announced he might still be. "Hard to tell the direction, but this damned place attracts all kinds of people. I boarded up the windows more than a year ago."

"We heard it wasn't sold after the foreclosure," Marty said.

"Wasn't. I live a quarter mile closer to town. Don't want hoodlums hanging out up here." He smiled, grimly. "Last Halloween, bunch of people in costumes came out here. I stayed out of sight and fired a couple shots in the air."

"And they left?" Digger asked.

"Yep. Word gets around. Haven't seen anyone for months. Until today. What were you doing up here?"

Digger took a deep breath. "Long story." She looked across Samuel to Marty. "You like telling stories."

He gave Samuel the basics, leaving out any speculation about who might have put anything in the small space. "Would you call that a mine or a cave?" he asked.

Samuel shrugged. "The Bloomington mines were not too far northwest of here, but they were early ones. About 1870s or 1880s. Long gone."

Digger said, "This didn't look like it had ever been mined, more like somebody dug into the earth to get at some coal."

Samuel grinned.

"Okay, that's mining. But I meant it didn't look, I don't know, formal."

"Coal runs all through here. Dirty work, but some people'd scrounge some from their own property. Would've been a long time before this house was built, I'd think."

"Somebody found the space." Marty nodded toward the hill. "It looked like it had been shorn up with two-by fours, at least for the part I could see."

Samuel nodded. "Have to be or it would have caved in long ago."

"Did you know the Jones family?" Digger asked.

"Met 'em. Tried to get a contract to do their yard work, but I guess I wasn't suitable for them."

Digger smiled. "Do you mow around the house?"

"Noticed that, did you? Yeah. Left it long for a while, but it encourages snakes and rats."

A shout from the hill made them turn toward it. The young deputy who'd directed Digger and Marty into the Quiet Spring building pointed behind the huge rock, and two other deputies moved toward him from the area near the window.

"Guess they found the way in," Samuel said.

After another ten minutes, the sheriff started down the hill, while the deputies began winding yellow crime scene tape by the entrance and several feet out.

Digger's frantic feeling increased. Uncle Benjamin had lifted an arm and waved one time, but that was all she'd seen. She blinked. Unknown to Sheriff Montgomery, Uncle Benjamin had attached himself to the man's leg as he walked toward the house.

SAMUEL HAD HEADED HOME after a handshake with Sheriff Montgomery, but Digger and Marty now sat in a small conference room in the Oakland law enforcement building. She'd been in what she'd heard referred to as the sheriff's satellite office in Maple Grove, but never in here. She thought there was a jail, or at least holding cells in this place. She didn't like the thought.

They'd barely spoken since they left the old Jones property. Marty glanced toward the closed door. "What the hell did you see up there?"

"See?"

"Don't give me crap, Digger. You either thought you saw your uncle, or you pray to him."

She stared at him, not sure what he meant.

"When we were behind that rock, you stood up for a second and screamed, 'Oh God. Uncle Benjamin.' What did you see?"

From where he lay curled up on the conference table, the very pale image of Uncle Benjamin spoke. *"You should tell him."*

Digger shook her head. "I can't."

"Why not?"

Sheriff Montgomery came in with Charlie Collins, who had helped at the Ancestral Sanctuary after Uncle Benjamin died. They sat across from Digger and Marty, and Montgomery opened a folder. He took out a photocopy of part of the plat map of the county. "Digger, staff from the zoning office say you were interested in this part of the county."

"I was."

Marty's eyes widened.

Montgomery pushed the paper across the table. "What did you want to know?"

"People talk about what happened to Daniel Stevens's car, that it would be harder to hide than a body. I wanted to see if there'd ever been an old mine near there. There wasn't."

"Yet you found someone's self-made seam."

She nodded.

He turned to Marty. "Same interest?"

He nodded. "We talked about it, but didn't really expect to find anything. It just seemed worth looking around with that metal detector."

"Did you go in the house?" Charlie asked.

They both shook their heads. Digger again looked at Uncle Benjamin. He appeared slightly more alert.

"Isn't it locked?" Marty asked.

Charlie said, "By the bank that owns the place. They don't want anyone in there."

Sheriff Montgomery leaned back in his chair. "Do you have any idea who would take a shot at you?"

Marty shook his head. "I don't write the kinds of articles that would annoy people that much."

The sheriff smiled slightly. "Says you. Digger?"

"You know the last time anyone shot at me, and that person's behind bars."

Before the sheriff could speak again, Marty asked. "Can you say what you found?"

"Not fool enough to go in without some kind of inspection first. Couple bushes near that rock are in front of a boarded hole that would let someone crawl in. Probably used to be bigger."

"When we looked in the window, we saw a suitcase and car parts," Digger said.

The sheriff stood and Charlie followed suit. "This is an active investigation, and you will not talk about it. Whoever put those items there is likely dead, but clearly there's a current criminal who wanted to keep it hidden. You can go home."

Before he walked out, he turned to them. "Do you know what today is?"

They looked at each other and Digger shook her head.

Marty said, "Damn. November 22nd."

"That's right. Fifty-seven years since my grandmother's brother died. You two may have helped her get some peace, but you could have been killed in the process."

A few seconds after the men left the room, Digger and Marty stood. He moved to the door, but stopped when he realized Digger had not followed him. "Come on."

Her voice choked. "Can you leave me alone for a minute?"

"Sure." He left, but didn't quite pull the door shut.

"Get closer and I'll try to crawl on your back."

"Can I drop you?"

He chuckled. *"I don't think so."*

She stooped and picked him up like a weightless baby, and he crawled on her back. When she moved toward the door, Marty stood there.

"You have some explaining to do."

CHAPTER TWENTY-FIVE

MARTY STARED STRAIGHT AHEAD as he drove. "Do I need to check you in someplace?"

"Ask him if he's talking about a luxury resort."

Digger smiled slightly. "I can see why'd you think that."

She looked down at Deep Creek Lake as they drove over it. Everything looked so normal. So peaceful. Nothing was. Would she lose Uncle Benjamin a second time?

"You're either delusional or you need to tell me who, or what, you're talking to."

"I don't know any more ways to tell you I can't do that."

"Then let's have a quiet ride home."

By the time they got to the Ancestral Sanctuary, Uncle Benjamin could float around the back seat. Digger had the impression he wouldn't have been able to go through the door. When she opened the passenger door he glided to the front and out.

She got out, and with the car door ajar, looked at Marty. "I'm sorry."

He turned. "You need to be able to trust your friends."

"I trust you."

"Wish I could say it was mutual. Shut the door, will you?"

She did.

Digger wasn't much of a crier, but she sat on the living room couch and sobbed.

Uncle Benjamin sat next to her with his head in his hands.

After a few minutes, she looked at him. "It's not your fault."

"You should have told him. Why didn't you tell him?"

She took a tissue from the box on the table and blew her nose. "Can you be sure you won't poof away if I tell someone about you?"

"I guess I don't know. But I also didn't know what would happen to me if I tried to shove you. It was worth it to try."

"But it almost killed you."

"If you want me to let a bullet get you next time, I can. But I wouldn't have anyone to drive me around."

DIGGER LEARNED THAT NEWS about old murders grabs the public's interest when they're connected to current crimes. The discovery of Daniel Stevens' car parts on the old Jones property fell into that category. Combined with Marilyn Jones Davis' admitting to the 'accidental' death of Nellie Porter, the press had a field day.

The Pittsburgh television stations and papers covered it well.

"I bet Marty wishes his paper came out more than once a week."

"He has an article on their web page."

"Not the same. Plus, you need a computer to read it."

Digger called Sheriff Montgomery on Monday to see if he knew who fired the shots at her and Marty.

"Leon Jones. Not a lot of people drove white Lincoln Navigators through Garrett County on Sunday, and several folks saw his yesterday afternoon. He said he was trying to scare you away."

"He just happened to be hanging around there with a rifle?"

"Apparently you talked to him about the property. Must have been one of those times you were not interfering in my investigation."

She ignored the comment. "And he carries a gun, a rifle, with him?"

"He doesn't have any registered firearms. This was a family heirloom, a Henry repeating rifle. One of the Kiwanis who marches in the Fourth of July Parade sometimes brings his for show."

Digger knew of the antique rifle, largely made for and used during the Civil War.

"But Leon brought it with him. That means he knew what was down there. I don't get it. He didn't have anything to do with Daniel Stevens' death."

"My guess is it had to do with what's in that suitcase. Which he says is none of my business." He chuckled. "If he hadn't taken pot shots at you, it wouldn't be my business."

THE UNSCHEDULED MURDER TRIP

MONDAY AFTERNOON, DIGGER drove to Oakland to visit Maryann Stevens Montgomery, who firmly believed Felicia Jones killed her brother. Felicia denied it, and said she had no idea how the car parts got in the mine seam on her family's former property. Then she moved out of the Quiet Spring.

Digger didn't doubt Felicia would have killed to prevent anyone from knowing her family had embezzled from the quarry. But the conversation with Harrison Hunter had led her to believe Harlan was likely the one who had sought out Daniel that night.

Digger looked around Maryann Stevens' peaceful living room and pushed aside the mug of tea she had been drinking. "I really thought Marilyn had fired those shots, but the sheriff said it was Leon."

"She had too much to lose."

"What do you mean?"

"First, she didn't kill Daniel, and if she knew anything it was decades afterwards." Maryann warmed to her topic. "She has a husband she probably loves, and she stands to inherit the quarry."

"No one ever talks about her mother, Suzi Jones."

Maryann waved a hand. "She's a spendthrift on the order of Felicia. She's never been involved in the business, or lived in that house in Bloomington. Like her daughter, if she learned anything, it was long after the murder."

"They should have spoken up."

"Yes, they should have."

"I keep trying to think of something I'm forgetting," Digger said.

"Close your eyes."

Digger did. It bothered her that a motive for Daniel's killing probably wouldn't be known. Felicia had said that the books were short. No records existed that far back...Digger's eyes flew open. "The suitcase."

"What suitcase?" Maryann asked.

"I just remembered that one was in the little cave with the car parts. I don't think it's mentioned in any of the news coverage." She wondered if it contained financial records. But why keep them for so long?

"Sometimes Roger doesn't tell everything he knows to the media."

Uncle Benjamin lay on Maryann's small dining table, which sat just outside the kitchen. He had gotten a lot better, but Digger wondered if he would ever get his full strength back.

"You know, it didn't look more than fifty years old. Maybe he's the one who hid it there.

She turned to say goodbye to Maryann, who stared at her intently. "What's wrong, Digger?"

"Oh? Nothing. Just a long couple days."

Maryann shook her head. "It's more than that."

Digger smiled. "I really do need to get back. I took off today, but I plan to go to work Tuesday." She shrugged into her coat.

"Thanks for coming. And say hello to Marty for me."

Digger wished she could.

CHAPTER TWENTY-SIX

TUESDAY, DOZENS OF FRIENDS and business acquaintances called You Think, We Design to see if Digger was okay. Holly joked that they had more free publicity than if she or Digger had designed the White House Christmas card.

A vastly improved Uncle Benjamin spent much of the day in the building's attic. He appeared as a Union soldier, George Washington, and finally Betsy Ross, sewing a flag.

"How do you think I look in a dress?"

Digger knew he wanted to cheer her up, but forced humor wasn't going to do it.

She decided to go home a little early and was in her car when Matthew Stevens called to ask if Digger could stop by. She felt exhausted and wanted to beg off, but didn't.

Sylvia and Brian greeted her at the door and made much over her experience on Sunday. Brian felt guilty about it. "If I'd never asked you to help find my grandfather, you wouldn't have been involved in any of this."

"I can't say I liked being shot at, but all in all, I'm glad Leon Jones implicated himself."

Sylvia led them into the living room where a gas fire gave the room a cozy feel. Matthew sat on one of the facing loveseats with his legs on an ottoman. His pallor said more about his illness than on prior visits.

"Digger, thanks for coming. I wanted to show you something. I gave Sheriff Montgomery a copy." He gestured with some papers he held to a spot next to him on the loveseat.

"Sure." She sat, and Sylvia and Brian sat across from her. She turned slightly so she could look at Matthew.

He handed her the top paper.

"That's what I saw on their dining room table the other day, before you rushed us out of here."

Digger studied it. The one-page profit and loss statement for Mountain Granite Quarry was for 1962. The firm cleared $22,000. Not a lot of money, but considering salaries and other expenses had been paid and there was no indication of debt, the company was moving in the right direction.

She looked up.

"My mother kept that in part because it became the basis for what she received when she sold out her half of the business. She also wanted my sister and me to have it because my dad's name is at the top, with that bastard Harlan Jones, as an owner."

Digger wasn't sure what to say, so she simply nodded.

Matthew continued. "One of the few things Leon Jones finally told Sheriff Montgomery is that he has, and I quote, 'reason to believe' that the suitcase you saw in the hole in the hill has papers about Mountain Granite Quarry from the 1960s."

"Did he say what they would show?" Digger asked.

"Only that his father did some creative accounting, but he didn't realize it until Felicia Jones told him to get rid of some records a number of years ago."

"So why didn't he?" she asked.

"He says he didn't want to get involved."

"He could have burned them," Digger said.

Matthew shrugged. "Felicia was, probably is, a difficult woman. Maybe those papers gave him something to hold over her head."

Digger nodded slowly. "That makes a lot of sense. He didn't want to risk anyone finding out the quarry cheated Isabella, so he thought he hid them where only he could get at them."

Sylvia nodded. "Something like that. I bet he was afraid Isabella's heirs could probably get some restitution."

Digger handed the paper back to Matthew. "Are you going to try to do that?"

"I'm not sure I want to prolong all this. And it would probably put the quarry out of business. I think nine or ten people work there."

"That's a lot of jobs," she said.

"It is. What I want is for all of this to come out. Make sure that everyone knows what happened to my dad, and why."

Brian spoke. "And that any rumors about him stealing from the company aren't true."

Digger smiled at him. "And they'll know that because of you."

AT FIVE-THIRTY, SHE finished a short phone call with her parents. As always, their solution to any problem in her life was that she move to the Gulf Coast of Florida, where they had retired.

Digger used her consistent response, that she wouldn't live anywhere that had palm trees instead of evergreens. And now she had the Ancestral Sanctuary to care for. She invited her parents to come north for Christmas. Not likely they would.

Next on her list was Franklin. She'd talked to him briefly Sunday night, but pled exhaustion. He'd read what happened on the *Maple Grove News* website, so at least she didn't have to explain everything.

"I don't know, cuz. It seems as if when I leave town you get shot at."

"Tell him he should come home more often."

"Be glad you aren't around when it happens."

"What I am glad about is that you were with Marty. I'd hate to think of you being alone on that deserted property."

Digger couldn't tell him that Uncle Benjamin had probably saved her life with his push. Franklin would think she hit her head.

She watched the six o'clock news and ate a frozen dinner. She decided to treat herself and took a brownie mix out of the pantry. She'd bake them and take most of them to work on Wednesday.

She had just placed them in the oven when the doorbell rang. Through the glass in the door she could see Marty.

"It's about time he showed up."

"Maybe it's about time for you to vanish."

"I never listen to your private conversations. Come on, Ragdoll." Uncle Benjamin floated up the main staircase to the second floor.

Digger felt like a girl with her first high school crush. She told herself all she wanted was an amicable conversation so she didn't feel awkward when she ran into Marty around town. She opened the door.

"Hey, Digger. Can I come in?"

"Sure." She let him in and shut the door. "Come on into the living room."

As she sat on the couch, he handed her something small and cylindrical.

She stared at it. "A bullet. Is this supposed to bring fond memories?"

"It's from the twenty-one gun salute the military did when my grandfather's brother was buried at Arlington National Cemetery. They let you keep the shells if you want them."

"Thanks. I'll treasure this."

He sank into his spot at the opposite end of the couch. "Did you consider that Maryann Stevens minds a lot of other people's business?"

Digger grunted. "I guess in this case it let her know about her brother. And she's getting to know Matthew and his family."

He pushed his glasses back on his nose. "She also thinks you miss me."

"You do, you know."

Digger shut her eyes for a moment and tilted her head back. When she opened them, he had a slight smile. She stood.

Marty's expression changed. "Are you throwing me out?"

She tilted her head toward the hallway. "You've got a heavy coat. Come out to the family plot with me."

"I have some pretty vivid memories of the last time I was out there."

She walked to the front hall and took her coat off the rack. Bitsy, sensing a good time, barked. "Okay, you can come, too." He bounded for the back door.

They walked in silence over the dry leaves, up the rise toward the graves, and passed under the metal arbor with the Browning name on it.

Digger stopped in front of Uncle Benjamin and Aunt Clara's stone, the most modern one in the little cemetery. "Do you believe people can come back?"

THE UNSCHEDULED MURDER TRIP

Marty stood next to her and stared at the headstone. "I've only recently considered the idea."

"I don't know a lot about it, and I'm not sure what happens if you talk about it. Does the person disappear if you tell someone? Do you get put in an institution because people think you're crazy?"

Marty turned toward her and then looked back at the stone. "I take it the person can go where they want."

"Not as much as you'd think. Apparently, they have to stay in their former residence or can only leave it with the person who lives there."

"Brings new meaning to the phrase 'close family ties.'"

Digger smiled. "It does. Sometimes too close."

Marty frowned. "Do they uh, hang out with you 24/7? That could be…awkward."

"They can be considerate about privacy. Sometimes."

Marty turned to go back to the house. "It's cold out here."

Digger kept pace with him. Bitsy ran ahead. On the porch, Ragdoll sat on the rail and Uncle Benjamin stood behind her.

Some time, she might have to make a hard decision. Let Uncle Benjamin go, or live most of her life by herself. But not tonight. Tonight she'd sit in front of the fire with a good friend she hoped might become more than that.

THE END

ABOUT THE AUTHOR

Elaine L. Orr writes four mystery series, including the thirteen-book Jolie Gentil cozy mystery series, set at the Jersey shore. Two of her books (including *Behind the Walls* in the Jolie series) have been finalists for the Chanticleer Mystery and Mayhem Awards.

Unscheduled Murder Trip, second in the Family History Mystery Series, received an Indie B.R.A.G Medallion. Other books are in the River's Edge Series (set in rural Iowa) and the Logland Series (set in small-town Illinois).

She also writes plays and novellas. A member of Sisters in Crime, Elaine grew up in Maryland and moved to the Midwest in 1994. She enjoys meeting readers at events throughout the country.

Scan this QR code to visit my Author Page.

www.amazon.com/stores/Elaine-L.-Orr/author/B001HD0X6K

Authors always appreciate reviews. If you enjoyed *The Unscheduled Murder Trip*, please post a review on your favorite web site or mention it on Instagram or Facebook, Let your local bookstore or library know that you liked a book. You can also contact Elaine to see if she would be available in person or via Zoom to talk to your community or book group.

Scan this QR code to leave a review on Amazon.com

Amazon.com/review/create-review?&asin=B08PT2DKY5

www.elaineorr.com | www.elaineorr.blogspot.com

elaineorr55@yahoo.com

Printed in Great Britain
by Amazon